MYS

OF THE DEEP

MYSTERIES OF THE DEEP

Compiled & edited by Frank Spaeth from the files of FATE Magazine

Bounty Books

"Reprinted from"
MYSTERIES OF THE DEEP

GALDE PRESS, INC.,
Lakeville MN 55044 USA

This edition published 2005 by Bounty Books,
a division of Octopus Publishing Group Ltd
2-4 Heron Quays, London E14 4JP

ISBN 0 7537 1116 8
ISBN13 9780753711163

A CIP catalogue record for this book is available from the British Library

Printed and bound in Great Britain by
Mackays of Chatham plc, Chatham, Kent

Table of Contents

Gigantic Ocean Creatures

Bermuda Triangle Mysteries

Atlantis: Land Under the Sea

Other Ocean Oddities

Introduction

Two-thirds of the Earth's surface is covered by water. It surrounds continents and divides nations. People around the world depend on bodies of water for their lives and livelihoods. Much of the struggle for international power in the past was over which country would control these waterways. Explorers were sent in gigantic sea-going vessels to find out all they could about the world via its oceans, seas, lakes, and rivers. Yet, despite all of the expeditions and adventures across oceans and seas over the centuries, the deep is still filled with mysteries and unexplained phenomena. Many water-covered areas of the Earth have never been explored. No one knows for certain what the oceans and seas may be hiding.

Since 1948, FATE magazine has reported true stories about the strange and unknown, including a number of features dealing with these mysteries of the deep. FATE has presented articles on everything from the Loch Ness Monster to Giant Jellyfish, and from Atlantis to the Bermuda Triangle. The stories have ranged from thoroughly detailed investigations to brief personal experiences. In all cases, the authors use their own perspectives to try to make some sense of the unknown lurking in our world's waterways.

I have been enthralled by the ocean since I was a small child. I have often marveled at the strength and power of those mighty waters, and I have had the opportunity to behold many great bodies of water, from the Pacific to the Atlantic, and from the Gulf of Mexico to the North Sea. I thoroughly researched the annals of FATE to find the "best of the best" from nearly fifty years of the world's leading paranormal and supernatural publication. There was more information available about the many strange experiences the lakes, seas, and oceans of the world have given us than I could even begin to put into this compilation.

While researching this book I uncovered many interesting and thought-provoking articles and side notes. For instance, at the end of one of the Bermuda Triangle articles I found a note stating that the magazine had received a letter, dated April 4, 1975, from the large insurance firm, Lloyd's of London. The letter asserted in part, ". . . it may interest you to know that our intelligence service can find no evidence to support the claim that the 'Bermuda Triangle' has more losses than elsewhere. This finding is upheld by the United States Coast Guard whose computer records of casualties in the Atlantic go back to 1958." Yet, even apparent facts such as this one have not stopped people from investigating this, and other, supposed mysterious phenomena. That is one thing that makes matters of the strange and unknown so interesting to follow. Each individual must ultimately decide what to believe in regard to unexplained incidents, based on their own personal experiences and the experiences of others.

Through my research I have tried to share a wide range of thoughts, experiences, and ideas, while making sure the basic facts of each mysterious phenomenon have been covered. I have taken articles from issues as recent as summer of 1995, and others dating back to the early days of FATE. Some of the articles come from authors well known to many decades of FATE readers, including Martin Caidin, Dr. Karl P. N. Shuker, and Jerome Clark. Other articles share personal experiences with phenomena including ghost ships and other unexplained oceanic occurrences by people who may not be experts in the field of paranormal activity.

I think the article selections in this book are as interesting and diverse as those of you who read FATE magazine. I hope you enjoy perusing the contents of this compilation as much I enjoyed putting it together. Most of all, I hope that *Mysteries of the Deep* will become an important addition to your collection of books on mysterious phenomena.

—Frank Spaeth
Associate Editor
FATE Magazine

Mysterious Ships and Shipwrecks

On Board with John Wayne's Ghost

William G. Roll

December 1994

In August 1979, at 4:00 A.M., Hutchins had his first encounter with what he believes is John Wayne's ghost.

"I don't want to change anything," Lynn Hutchins told me. "I want to leave it the way it is. The way John had it."

Hutchins, a Los Angeles lawyer, had bought John Wayne's yacht, *The Wild Goose*, in June 1979, about a month before Wayne's death. Within four weeks, John Wayne had returned.

I was in California attending a conference and used the opportunity to conduct an investigation. I was surprised to discover that this handsome old yacht had been a World War

II mine sweeper, and I was even more surprised that she had an identical twin, the famed *Calipso*. The lives of twins often run parallel, and it seemed right that both boats should be explorers, one of the waters of this world, the other of the world of spirits. One was captained by a living adventurer, Jacques Cousteau, and the other, perhaps, by a ghost.

The solid double hull of the *Calipso*—built to withstand exploding mines—was ideally suited to navigate coral reefs and Arctic icebergs. *The Wild Goose*'s same rugged construction and wartime service appealed to John Wayne. And, at 140 feet, it was large enough for him to add staterooms and bedrooms for himself and his guests.

Hutchins could barely believe his good fortune in acquiring *The Wild Goose*. His emotional attachment to the yacht began from the time he learned of her availability. Negotiations for the purchase had not been easy. Wayne, working through his son, Michael, interrogated Hutchins at great length about his philosophical and political views. Finally these were deemed to be compatible with Wayne's own world views. Hutchins was considered suitable to be the boat's next owner. Both Hutchins and Wayne seemed to regard the change of ownership as something of a ceremonial event.

The Wild Goose was not just a boat. It was "John's boat," said Hutchins, and he invested his heart and soul into it, as well as a great deal of money.

Hutchins kept his word to keep the boat just as Wayne had left it. Wayne's books are still in the library, and plaques and awards he received still hang in the main salon. Hutchins asked for and received permission to keep them on board. When I visited *The Wild Goose* in January 1983, I found a floating museum tended by a doting caretaker, Lynn Hutchins, who took special pride in his charge.

Shopping for John Wayne

Within a month of Wayne's death, Hutchins began to feel that Wayne was trying to get him to do things he wanted done on board. "Like someone is ordering me to do it," said Hutchins. He showed me a pair of brass lamps that he felt compelled to buy for the galley when he saw them at a marine store in June 1979.

When he had hung them in place, he told me, a crew member who had been with Wayne for fifteen years saw them and claimed that the same type of lamps had been in those same places before. They were taken down because Wayne kept hitting his head on them, but they were still stored on board. The crew member showed them to Hutchins. The old lamps used kerosene while the new ones were electrical, but in every other way they were identical.

"I hung them in the same place he had them, the same spot, the same nail," Hutchins said. "The man's getting me to do his shopping for him."

In August 1979, at 4:00 A.M., Hutchins had his first encounter with what he later came to regard as Wayne's ghost.

"As I turned from the toilet to walk out of the master bath back to the master stateroom, it was just dawn. I could see this big, tall figure, this fellow standing right there in the doorway. He took the whole doorway, to the master bath. He was standing by the big porthole, three feet back of the doorway, with a little bit of a smile on his face."

Hutchins thought the figure was a real person and started toward it though it seemed twice his size. But, "he just vanished like that."

The sighting lasted three to four seconds. The figure, Hutchins said, wore a cowboy hat that shadowed its facial features. I asked Hutchins if it could have been a crew member dressed up that way. Hutchins was sure it wasn't. The crew members were in their quarters below. Besides, the figure vanished too quickly for it to have been a real person.

The next apparitional episode came a couple of months later in October 1979. This time it was 4:00 P.M. Hutchins was in the main salon, sitting at a poker table, facing the bar. He got up and went to the bar to pour himself a drink. The bar had mirrored walls.

"I looked right behind me (through the mirror). Standing by the chair I'd just gotten out of was a tall figure, all gray, wearing a wide-brimmed hat and Western garb. I couldn't see his face, but that was twenty feet away. I thought to myself as I stood there, 'How in hell did he get in here?'"

Hutchins said he started to speak to the figure when it vanished. The sighting had lasted four to five seconds.

There was another strange feature to this episode. Just prior to the sighting Hutchins heard a clinking sound from the bar. The beer mugs, tightly bound together to prevent breakage at sea, were moving against each other.

Six to nine months after taking possession of *The Wild Goose*, Hutchins began to hear footsteps on the deck whenever he spent a night on board, which was about a dozen times in 1982. The pattern was always the same. Around 2:00 to 2:30 A.M. he would hear a "clump, clump, clump, like someone walking like they've got lead in their shoes, up and down this deck up here past the stateroom. It walked by, and a short time later it's clump, clump, clump coming back."

At first, Hutchins thought it was an inconsiderate crew member. On the third occasion, he decided to find out who it was. "I was out of the door in five seconds when the sound started," he said. "I'm fast. I ran down this whole deck and all along the other deck. There was nothing. Everything was locked up; the crew was fast asleep. No one had time to get off the boat."

This had been going on for a year when Hutchins learned from a crew member who had spent many years on the boat that it was Wayne's habit to walk twenty laps around the deck in the evening. This was the first time Hutchins had heard about Wayne's nightly exercise.

Hutchins kept the incidents to himself. He had not spoken of them to C. B., the caterer for a wedding reception on the yacht. C. B., who spent the night on board, also reported hearing footsteps.

A Protective Spirit

Hutchins was now convinced that the spirit of John Wayne was on his boat. There was nothing scary about this presence. On the contrary, Hutchins experienced a feeling of protective warmth in the master stateroom, and C. B. had a general feeling of being protected on the boat.

In February 1980, an incident occurred that received wide media coverage, convincing Hutchins that John Wayne was not only on board his old boat but in charge of it, too. *The Wild Goose* was in Newport Harbor. Wayne's house was also located there, facing the basin.

The boat was again host to a catered wedding reception, and approximately eighty people were on board. *The Wild Goose* was not docked. It was out in the harbor, riding on its own power against a strong wind.

Suddenly the engines cut off, apparently because of a crew member's error. A dead engine can be extremely dangerous in a small, congested harbor like Newport. Without engines to provide navigational control, *The Wild Goose* could drift freely and cause substantial damage, since it takes several minutes for the engines to be restarted.

There was a long delay and the boat drifted, but not in a haphazard way. According to Hutchins, the boat moved against the 40-knot wind and the ocean-going tide, to head straight for John Wayne's house.

"We drifted in sideways and sidled in the mud right in front of John's house," Hutchins told me. None of the adjacent docks or boats were damaged or even touched in the incident.

A Miraculous Occurrence?

The occurrence may not have been quite as miraculous as it seemed. Although the news media played up the story of Wayne's boat heading home, and although *The Wild Goose* did, in fact, settle in front of Wayne's house, there is some controversy about how this happened.

B. M., a crew member who had been on the bridge at the time, disagreed with Hutchins' version of the incident. B. M. told me that the 40-knot wind was directed at Wayne's house, not away from it, and that there was little tidal current in the basin at the time. B. M. thought that the strong wind could also have affected the current so that it also aimed toward the house.

Just as Hutchins' version must be viewed in light of his conviction that John Wayne was back in charge of his boat, so B. M.'s report should perhaps be tempered by the fact that, according to Hutchins, B. M. had been fired, since he was the officer in charge when the engines cut off. In any case, it remains interesting that the stopping of the engines, the wind, and the current all combined to bring the boat to where it landed.

In January 1983, four psychics from the Patricia Hayes School of Inner Sense Development attempted to communicate with John Wayne's spirit. Hutchins hoped to verify his experiences and to know if there was anything Wayne wanted from him.

A TV company arranged for the psychics to participate and asked me to come, too. I had worked with Patricia before and welcomed the opportunity to do so again.

In addition to Patricia, three psychics took part: William Clema, Janice Hayes, and Ester-Elke Kaplan. During two psi scans, the psychics walked around the boat attempting to pick up impressions of psychically active areas. This was followed by a psi session or seance, in which they sought to communicate with whatever spirit entities were present. Hutchins had not told the psychics about his experiences.

In the initial psi scan of the boat, three of the psychics reported getting strongly negative feelings in the crew's quarters below deck. Janice Hayes had the added impression of a problem with a younger crew member who in some way had been hard to control.

B. M., who had served with Wayne for twenty years, later reported that in 1964 a young deckhand, two Mexican boys, and the visiting son of Wayne's valet took a plywood skiff eight miles down the Mexican coast one night, against the captain's orders. On the return trip the boat overturned. The deckhand and the Mexican boys drowned. Only the valet's son survived.

Also during the psi scan, Kaplan reported that the second guest bedroom contained "lots of fun energy and mischief. Someone was sick here for a while."

She added that a nurse had slept in the room. I learned that a nurse had indeed occupied that room, along with

Wayne's young son, Ethan, to whom she served as a companion. According to a crew member, Ethan was full of mischief and energy. Though it was possible that he had been sick at some time, there was no record of this. Perhaps Kaplan saw an image of the nurse and from this concluded that someone had been ill.

The master bedroom and the passage to the bathroom were identified as active areas by the psychics. This was where Hutchins had his first apparitional experience.

Psychic Messages

During the psi session the message "Tell Lady I love her" was received as a communication from Wayne. Lady was Wayne's pet name for Pat Stacey, with whom he had a longstanding personal relationship.

Patricia Hayes received the impression that Wayne had a hearing problem in his right ear. This was corroborated by B. M., who who said that Wayne had a persistent fungus in that ear that could have affected his hearing.

Hayes also received an impression of an old crew member in his fifties or sixties who had been intimately associated with *The Wild Goose*. This may relate to Peter Stein, captain of *The Wild Goose* until his death at age sixty-five. B. M. said that Old Pete, as he was called, used to tell great sailor's yarns, and that he and Wayne often talked and drank together before Stein died of a heart attack in 1969. Wayne was very fond of this colorful character, according to B. M.

What does *The Wild Goose* tell us? Did Hutchins simply have an overactive imagination that made him see and hear things that weren't there? Did the psychics only bring up things that might be true about the crew of any old boat or that they knew about Wayne from having read or heard about him?

Hutchins scored very moderately (21) on Wilson and Barber's inventory of the fantasy-prone personality, a fact that weighs against the likelihood that the sightings and footsteps were the products of an overactive imagination. The psychics, for their part, did not believe they could have known the things they said about Wayne and the boat, even subconsciously; and some of their impressions, like the remarks about Lady and the nurse, seemed more than chance hits.

Assuming that the facts cannot be dismissed in these ways, does this mean that John Wayne had returned from the other world to continue his journey on his old boat and with his old traveling companions?

There is another possibility.

If we are to understand psychic phenomena, it is not enough to look at them just as phenomena. It is not enough to know that there were apparitions, footsteps, and other incidents on *The Wild Goose* that might be related to John Wayne. We also need to look at Lynn Hutchins, the person at the center of the occurrences.

You could not be with Hutchins without becoming aware of his emotional attachment to Wayne. When Hutchins spoke about Wayne, he spoke about family. When he spoke about *The Wild Goose*, he spoke about his and Wayne's family home.

Boats promote family feelings. There are good reasons for this: to deal with the elements without, the crew needs to act as a single, coordinated body. This feeling of one body and one mind is one of the delights of being at sea. But here the head of the family, the real captain of the boat, was missing.

A Captain's Protection

To Hutchins' affection for Wayne was added his need for a captain who would look after the ship and protect it in crises of wind and weather. Is it possible that Hutchins' attachment to Wayne, combined with the need for his protective presence, evoked that presence?

The time Hutchins must have felt he and *The Wild Goose* were most in need of their captain, when the boat was drifting dangerously in Newport harbor, was also the time Wayne seemed most decisively to take charge. Hutchins' apparitional experiences, his and C. B.'s sense of a protective presence, and the footsteps they heard where Wayne had walked, were now solidly identified for Hutchins as Wayne's own.

But why the ghost's cowboy hat and Western garb? Wayne surely would not have worn those at sea. Psychic images are rarely photographic reflections of reality. The intention behind the impression is what counts, and this is usually to provide information. The apparitions, footsteps, and other incidents said that Wayne was on board—but was the message sent by Wayne or by Hutchins?

The Return of the Dead

The return of the dead is most often experienced among the people and places that surrounded them in life. Hutchins did not know Wayne directly, but he possessed *The Wild Goose* with all its memorabilia, visible and invisible.

The invisible traces of Wayne would have included place memories. It seems that events not only leave their traces in a person's brain but also in the things and places where the events took place.

If the person has died and if the trace results in an image of the person in physical space, it may be mistaken for that person's spirit. These traces are called place memories and may be remembered by other people who come in contact with them, assuming some psychic sensitivity.

A psychic, like the members of the Hayes group, is a person who can call on this sensitivity most hours of the day while the rest of us may only show evidence of being psychic at certain times. One of these times is late night-early morning, when a hormone, nocturnal melantonin, reduces the usual inhibition of the brain and we may see and hear things of which we are usually unaware. This impressionable time was when Hutchins had one of his apparitional experiences and when he habitually heard the footsteps.

Was the Wayne entity only a place memory evoked by an aroused brain? The fact that the footsteps were heard independently by another person, C. B., suggests that they were objectively real. The sense of purpose and protection associated with the presence also seem more than recalls of past events. But was it Wayne's spirit or Hutchins' that animated the presence?

It is fairly common for people to project their mental images into their surroundings. We call such images hallucinations when only the person himself or herself can see them. When other people experience the image the person projects, this may be a form of telepathy, and when the image appears solid, a form of psychokinesis (PK). Other terms for PK projections are materializations or thought forms.

There are stories of individuals who deliberately created a thought form of another person, where this thought form then acted more or less independently of its producer, sometimes being mistaken for a real person. It is probably more common for the process to be subconscious and to take place when someone has a strong need for someone else—who may then appear as a thought form. I believe that in some cases of haunting, we may be dealing with thought forms, and that the ghost of John Wayne could be an example.

The Titanic: A Disaster Foreseen?

George M. Behe

December 1994

Was the fate of the mighty Titanic *predicted in a novel? Many mysteries surround the death of one of the world's most famous ships.*

She has lain in dark silence for three quarters of a century now, lost in her memories, a prisoner of the ivy blackness that surrounds her. But she is not alone, for she did not die alone. Her death throes claimed the lives of two-thirds of her passengers and crew—1,500 people whose presence was felt by the explorers who finally discovered her resting place. Torn in half, she now lies on the seabed, her innards scattered around her in the desolation.

Once she was a queen, the largest and most beautiful ship in the world. A few lucky people can still remember viewing her magnificence with their own eyes. Fewer still are those who sailed on her and were lucky enough to survive. But everyone, even today, recognizes her name.

She was the *Titanic*.

The month of April 1912 was a high point in the annals of the White Star Line, one of Britain's leading steamship lines. RMS *Titanic*, the newest addition to their stable of thoroughbreds, was about to enter service as a carrier of passengers and mail. She was the largest moving object ever created by the hands of humans—882 feet long, 92 feet wide, 46,000 tons. A double bottom had been built into her hull, with transverse watertight bulkheads spaced along her length dividing her into sixteen watertight compartments. These, it was felt, would be more than enough to ensure the ship's safety in the event of a mishap. Any water that somehow managed to get through the double bottom and enter the hull would be contained in one of these compartments, allowing the rest of the ship to continue normal operations.

An Accident? Unthinkable!

The mere sight of the *Titanic* was enough to inspire total confidence. Her four great funnels towered into the sky, a symbol of the final mastery of humankind over Nature. A serious accident to the ship was unthinkable. Indeed, her master, Captain Edward J. Smith, has been quoted as saying, "Modern shipbuilding has gone beyond that."

The British Board of Trade seems to have complacently agreed with him; their lifeboat regulations, long out of date, required that any ship of 10,000 tons or more must carry only sixteen wooden lifeboats. The *Titanic*, at 46,000 tons, was carrying the required sixteen boats, with an additional four Englehardt "collapsible" boats thrown in for good measure.

Its total lifesaving capacity was 1,178 people. The *Titanic* was certified to carry a maximum of 3,000 people, but no one seems to have given much thought to this enormous deficiency in lifesaving equipment. Word of mouth had it that the great vessel was unsinkable, so what was the use of cluttering up the deck with more lifeboats?

A single look at the sumptuous public rooms on the great vessel made one almost forget that they were even on a ship. What could possibly go wrong?

Predictions of Doom

Yet, there were people who became absolutely certain that something was going to happen to the *Titanic* on her maiden voyage. Although a few of these people had no direct connection with the ship, others were among those who had booked their passage on the great liner. Of the latter, several people actually canceled their passage, preferring to take any other ship rather than sail on the *Titanic.* Others, in spite of grave misgivings, retained their bookings for the maiden voyage of the great vessel. Many paid for that decision with their lives when the *Titanic* foundered after striking an iceberg in the mid-Atlantic.

The best-known "premonition" of the *Titanic* disaster was probably not a premonition at all. It occurred in 1898, fourteen years before the maiden voyage of the *Titanic*, and, on the surface, bears striking similarities to what actually befell the great liner.

This "premonition" came in the form of a novel by Morgan Robertson titled *Futility*, which told the story of the *Titan*, the largest ship in the world. Her dimensions were roughly comparable to those of the real *Titanic*; her equipment was the most modern, her crewmen the best. The *Titan* set sail one April day with a full complement of passengers, but with insufficient lifeboats to accommodate everyone on board.

To help ensure a record crossing, great triangular sails had been hoisted on each of the *Titan*'s two masts. Her master was so intent on making a speed record that, when his vessel accidentally rammed a windjammer, no effort was made to stop and pick up survivors. One of the doomed sailors in the water shouted up a curse, calling on God to avenge the heartless behavior of the departing steamer.

Later, on a foggy but moonlit night, the *Titan* encountered an iceberg in the mid-Atlantic and was unable to turn in time to prevent a collision. The big steamer ran up onto the sloping shelf of an iceberg, sliding forward and upward onto the ice until she was almost completely out of the water. The vessel toppled heavily onto her starboard side, her machinery smashing down and rupturing her side plates. The *Titan* then slid back down the ice slope into the sea, her starboard lifeboats being smashed in the process. Only a handful of people survived when the vessel sank.

The above story about Robertson's fictional *Titan* is usually the first one trotted out by authors discussing psychic aspects of the *Titanic* disaster. Several bogus stories have arisen concerning the circumstances under which Robertson's novel was written. These usually claim that the author either dreamed the details of his novel or that he "went into a trance" and "saw" the events of the novel unfold, later writing the details down in the form of fiction. These tales are untrue. Robertson's novel was written in the same mundane manner so well understood by all authors as the "seat of the pants technique."

The similarities between Robertson's novel and the sinking of the *Titanic* are obvious, and many authors have played up these parallels through the years. Tables have even been compiled comparing the specifications of the two vessels and the circumstances of their sinkings. The similarities seem uncanny at first, but, when considered in a broader context, they are really perfectly understandable.

Morgan Robertson had wished to write about the greatest ship in the world, but he did not want his literary creation to be rapidly overtaken and outdated by new advances in shipbuilding. To avoid this, he simply projected the dimensions of his fictional ship a couple of steps ahead of the technology of 1898. By postulating a ship of a certain length, he could roughly calculate her tonnage, carrying capacity and other specifications. Although it thus becomes obvious that physical similarities between the *Titan* and the *Titanic* would be almost automatic, one glaring difference between the two ships is immediately apparent: Robertson still envisioned the continued use of auxiliary sail in steamers of the future, a characteristic which the *Titanic* did not possess.

As to the insufficient number of lifeboats on the fictional *Titan*, Robertson was utilizing a trend which was visible even in 1898. He knew of the lack of regulations governing an increase in the number of required lifeboats as ship sizes increased. The author merely projected this trend to its extreme, but logical, end result—namely, a huge liner foundering with too few boats to save her passengers.

The plot of Robertson's novel required that the *Titan* be destroyed very suddenly, with only a handful of survivors escaping the disaster. The author ruled out a storm at sea as being his instrument of destruction, since any storm capable of destroying the largest ship in the world would also destroy her lifeboats (along with the survivors necessary for the novel's conclusion). A collision with another ship was also ruled out, as was a shipboard fire, as these disasters would not have destroyed the *Titan* quickly enough (and would have introduced more lifeboats and survivors into the story, interfering with the ending which Robertson had planned for his novel).

It appears that a spectacular collision with an iceberg was the only mishap that Robertson could envision which might simultaneously destroy the *Titan* and still fulfill all of his plot requirements. Robertson himself was a seaman, and he knew how dangerous an iceberg in the shipping lanes could be. Indeed, this danger was merely confirmed in 1912 when an iceberg claimed the *Titanic* on her maiden voyage.

The most outstanding similarity between the *Titanic* and Robertson's fictional ship was the author's choice of the name "*Titan*." If he had instead christened his ship the *Neptune*, it is unlikely that many people would have recalled his novel fourteen years later when the *Titanic* went down. Indeed, this fortuitous choice of names is probably the only thing which rescued Robertson's novel from complete obscurity.

Although many odd coincidental occurrences (including the above novel) can be cited in relation to the *Titanic* disaster, other cases have origins which do not seem to be rooted in coincidence.

During the writing of my book, *Titanic: Psychic Forewarnings of a Tragedy*, I was able to compile a list of twenty-nine cases which I felt were possibly psychic in nature. I felt that an additional thirty-five accounts contained enough detail to be classed as probable psychic phenomena, with many of these cases being of a precognitive nature.

A Real Premonition

The remainder of this article will be devoted to the examination of one of these latter cases—a very poignant story involving the death of the percipient herself. The incident in question took place in Kirkendbright, Scotland, on the night of April 14,1912.

W. Rex Sowden was the captain in charge of the city's Salvation Army Corps, which had taken on the responsibility of caring for a little orphan girl named Jessie. The child was lying in bed dangerously ill, and it was necessary for someone to remain with her at all times to monitor her condition. Sowden knew this, and, on the night of April 14, he went to bed confident that the little girl was being properly looked after.

Shortly before 11:00 P.M. someone knocked desperately on Sowden's bedroom door, calling, "Will you please come at once, Captain? Jessie is dying."

Captain Sowden immediately got out of bed, dressed and hurried to the room of the little orphan girl. He sat at her bedside for a few minutes until, at exactly 11:00, Jessie suddenly sat up in her bed. When she saw Sowden sitting beside her, she begged him, "Hold my hand, Captain. I am so afraid. Can't you see that big ship sinking in the water?"

Sowden thought that the girl's mind was wandering, and he attempted to comfort her, telling her that she had been having a nightmare. Jessie knew better.

"No, the ship is sinking," she told him. "Look at all those people who are drowning . . . Wally is playing a fiddle and is coming to you."

To humor her, Captain Sowden looked around the room without seeing anything out of the ordinary. He gently laid the little girl back onto the bed, covered her again, and then watched as she lapsed into a coma.

Several hours went by while Captain Sowden sat faithfully by Jessie's bedside, but the child lay almost motionless beside him. Then, unexpectedly, Sowden heard the latch on the bedroom door move. Assuming that someone was coming to check on the little girl, the captain arose from his seat. Opening the bedroom door he was surprised to find the hallway empty, but then, quite suddenly, he had the eerie feeling that someone had moved past him and entered the bedroom.

Captain Sowden rushed back to Jessie's bedside and saw that the moment of crisis had arrived. Death was only a few moments away. The heartbroken man stood looking down at the little girl when she again opened her eyes and looked at him.

"My mother has come to take me to heaven," said Jessie quietly. Captain Sowden held her hand for a few moments, and the little girl then died peacefully.

As Captain Sowden rose slowly from the child's bedside, he again heard the latch on the bedroom door being lifted. Once again he found no one visible when he stepped into the hallway. Captain Sowden felt certain, though, that little Jessie and her mother had left the bedroom together.

The vision of the sinking ship which Jessie had experienced took place at 11:00 P.M. in Scotland. Allowing for the difference in longitude, this was about three and a half hours before the *Titanic* struck the iceberg. It seems clear that the little girl's experience was precognitive in nature, but what of her mention of the man named Wally who was playing a fiddle?

Captain Sowden soon learned that the leader of the *Titanic*'s band had been Wallace Hartley, whom he had known well as a boy. However, he had long ago lost track of Hartley and didn't know that "Wally" had gone to sea as a ship's bandsman. Therefore, it would seem that little Jessie's vision was clairvoyant as well as precognitive, for she had somehow known Hartley's first name.

Wallace Hartley and his fellow bandsmen on the *Titanic* had played their music to reassure the passengers around them. The musicians made no effort to save themselves, and they every one of them died. Somehow, little Jessie knew that Wally would not survive the catastrophe.

Later, in relating his account of little Jessie's vision, Captain Sowden made it very clear that he was deeply impressed by what he had witnessed.

"What I thought was hallucination," he said, "was a vision that stamped itself indelibly on my brain and changed my whole spiritual outlook."

If an impossible event actually does take place, we should expect very few people to have predicted that event before its occurrence. The exact opposite seems to have taken place concerning the historical event we have just discussed. Dozens of instances are on record concerning people who felt certain that something would happen to the "unsinkable" *Titanic* on her maiden voyage.

One or two correct predictions of this impossible event might conceivably be attributed to chance. But how many such predictions of an impossible event must come true before coincidence can be ruled out and foreknowledge accepted as a more likely explanation? You must decide that for yourself.

U.S. Navy Meets a Phantom Ship

Howard H. Brisbane

April 1962

The men aboard the destroyer saw and heard the old sailing ship—but the radar scope was strangely empty.

One hundred miles northwest of San Francisco, late in the war year of 1942, the aged Navy destroyer U.S.S. *Kennison* groped for the Golden Gate through dense fog. But before the *Kennison* would see the security of the harbor she was going to see the unseeable. At that very instant she was being maneuvered toward the first of what were to be two encounters with phantom ships of the fleet of shadows.

The radarman was standing by at his scope, alert for the series of blips that would indicate the Farallon Islands off the

Golden Gate. Already the men not on watch were showing symptoms of "channel fever"—pressing liberty blues and talking of reunions with their girls.

I was standing lookout on the galley deck of the *Kennison* that day. Forward, the outlines of the ship's bridge were indistinct. Aft, I could barely make out the straddle-legged figure of Tripod, the fire control man, on watch atop the after gun deck.

Then my thoughts of juicy steaks and pretty girls were interrupted by a faint hissing noise to port. It drew closer, louder; I could hear a series of splashes, then creaking and popping sounds. The sounds were tending aft. I pressed the "talk" button on the headphone to report that something was making noises down the port side.

Before I could speak the excited voice of Jack Cornelius, Torpedoman First Class, of Chicago, Illinois, came over the phone from the fantail, "Tripod, Tripod, look aft!" and as an afterthought, "Fantail to bridge!"

"Bridge, Aye."

"My God, Jack!" exclaimed Tripod. "I see something! But what is it?"

"I don't know, what I mean is, it's a ship but—"

"Bridge to fantail. Cornelius, what's going on back there?"

"A ship almost clipped our fantail, just missed us a few yards. It was a two-masted sailing ship."

"Aye." A pause as the bridge talker reported to the Officer-of-the-Deck. "What course is it on? Where would it be now?"

"A course of one-three-five relative. It's somewhere on the starboard quarter."

After a couple of minutes lapse, the OD's voice came on the phone. "Cornelius, did you say that ship was a double-masted sail job?"

"Yes, sir."

"That's odd. The radar scope is empty. A two-master, eh? They're kind of rare on the Coast these days."

"Sir, this one was very rare. There was no one on deck and the helm was not manned! I could see it from on top of the after deck house."

"What?"

"That's correct, sir, no one at the wheel."

This news spread like wildfire.

At noon chow all the boys ribbed Jack unmercifully for reporting a ghost ship. He took it good-naturedly. Later I talked with Jack and told him I had heard the bow wash of the ship and the creaking of rigging.

He elaborated on the sighting. He said that in the twenty to thirty seconds that the ship was in sight he saw that she was unpainted and her deck and rigging dilapidated. She was under full but ragged sail.

"Tripod and I saw it. You heard it," he said shivering slightly. "Of course, I was startled and scared at first because of the near collision but when I got a good look at her, I got the crawling creeps!"

Five months later, in April 1943, I was still aboard the *Kennison*, this time steaming on an easterly course approximately fifty miles west of San Diego. We were returning to port after convoying the troopship *Lurline*, Honolulu bound through the submarine belt.

The sea was table-top smooth; the night was cool and brilliantly starlit. Carlton Hanschel, of San Diego, and I were on the 2000-2400 lookout watch on the flying bridge, enjoying the beautiful night. I began a slow sweep of the horizon with binoculars and picked up the curling white bow wake of a vessel off the starboard bow. Focusing above the wake, I made out the silhouette of a Liberty freighter. It was on an opposing course from the *Kennison*, steaming westward.

"Ship out there, Henschel," I commented.

He raised his glasses. "Yep, got her. Radar has been probably tracking her for twenty miles and the OD is just waiting to chew us out if we don't report it."

I reported to the bridge, "Ship bearing zero-four-five; target angle same; range, one-five-double-0 yards."

I could hear the bridge talker reporting to the OD, Lt. (jg) Richard Young, of Berkeley, California, in the wheel house directly below.

The OD stepped out on the starboard side of the bridge and cracked the door of the radar shack. "Hey, radar, wake up in there!" he called. "There just happens to be a Liberty ship on our starboard bow and not a word do I hear from you."

"Mr. Young, there also just happens to be nothing on radar," replied the watch in an irritated tone. "The scope is a complete blank."

Mr. Young went into the shack, where he remained for several minutes.

We did not challenge the vessel by signal light or radio because it was not Navy policy to challenge presumably friendly ships encountered outside the war zone. Actually, only in a dire emergency was a signal ever made, because of the submarine menace. It would have proved extremely interesting had this ship been challenged to identify herself.

I kept tracking the ship with binoculars and by using a trick of night vision—focusing my gaze to either side slightly, never directly at the freighter—I could see it with the naked eye.

Hanscbel and I started to resume our conversation but were interrupted by the OD. "Brisbane," he called from below me, "give me a check on that ship. I can't seem to find it now."

I raised the glasses to pinpoint the starboard beam. No, not there. A full minute passed as I searched, sector by sector, the entire starboard side.

"I can't find it, sir," I said sheepishly. "It's not there." Not thirty seconds elapsed since I had seen it, big and solid, through the glasses.

"That's silly! It's got to be there—I saw it. There are no fog banks, no blind spots on the horizon, no explosion, no SOS. Even if it turned away and steamed at top speed, we could still see it for several miles."

"Yes, sir."

Yes, I agree with that, I thought, but the ship has vanished!

The OD ordered all topside watchstanders to search carefully the entire 360 degrees of the horizon. One by one, they reported empty ocean.

Empty ocean—empty radar screens. Now twice the *Kennison*'s lookouts had sighted vessels that vanished from sight in scant seconds.

Our sightings might rationally be explained away as the result of unobserved malfunctions of the radars, or as mirages or derelicts. But as a witness who saw one ship, and heard the other, I say the evidence defies logical explanation.

I believe that the explanation for the shadow fleet, which sails in the tradition of the *Flying Dutchman*, lies in the area of psychic phenomena. Reports of these apparitions have been made by generations of responsible men. For example, from 1831 to 1865, 300 apparitions were sighted and recorded in the logs of ships by the observers.

Now the log is a document with a specific legal status, and shipmasters do not use its pages to record hearsay or tall tales. The log is for the truth as a mariner has seen it, and this is my log of the phantom ships that sailed alongside the U.S.S. *Kennison*.

Ghost Ship on the Goodwin Sands

Frank Madigan
June 1955

The American clipper crew saw the schooner smash up on the sands—yet no wreckage was found!

The most treacherous stretch of sands in the world are the Goodwins off the coast of Kent, England. The sands extend ten miles and are four miles wide. Lying not far from Deal, they have sunk hundreds of ships and claimed thousands of lives.

It is not surprising that there are stories of ghost ships seen in this region. However, it may seem surprising to some that these reports of phantom vessels must be true. They have been sighted too many times by too many reliable witnesses to be brushed away as imaginative tales.

There seems to be good reason to accept the phantom of the schooner *Lady Luvibund* without reserve also. This ship has a peculiar and tragic history. It perished on the Goodwin Sands on February 13, 1748. Ever since then, for more than 200 years, first class seamen, including ships' captains, have testified that they have seen a schooner, corresponding to the *Lady Luvibund*, with all sails set, go aground on the Goodwins. They have signed written statements, swearing they saw this ghost ship. Always, of course, after each such sighting a search has been made for survivors and wreckage but none ever has been found.

The *Lady Luvibund* has the unhappy distinction of being the only ship known to have been wrecked on the Goodwins deliberately. That is why this three-masted schooner went onto the sands with all sails set.

The vessel was under the command of Captain Simon Reed and was sailing for Oporto with a general cargo. When the vessel had sailed safely down the Thames from London, and since the night was perfectly calm and clear and the way ahead easy to navigate, the Captain handed over command to the first mate and went below to his cabin.

He was eager to do this because he was newly married, and together with his wife were her people and guests. They were celebrating the wedding. For the captain this was a honeymoon trip to Oporto. The cabin was gaily decorated and the wine flowed freely as the newly married couple was toasted again and again.

On deck, however, the first mate, John Rivers, was nursing a bitter jealousy and hatred for the captain. Simon Reed had stolen the girl John Rivers wanted to marry. Yet Captain Reed had no idea of this. So well, in fact, had the first mate concealed his feelings that he actually had served as best man at the wedding.

As he navigated the vessel, John Rivers was bitterly aware of the gaiety below. The sounds of it reached him on deck. Growing more and more agitated, he paced the deck, until his self-control broke completely. Snatching up a wooden belaying-pin from a rack, he crept up behind the man at the helm and struck him down, killing him instantly. Then seizing the helm, he swung it hard over, direct for the treacherous sands.

Suspicious of nothing and having every confidence in his first mate the Captain was too happy to notice the slight change in course. The *Lady Luvibund* raced into the sands at full speed, striking them in a welter of toppling masts and rending timbers.

The Captain and his guests were trapped below—drowned instantly. So complete was the disaster that by morning nothing remained of the schooner. The impact under full sail smashed her to pieces and the tides dispersed the fragments.

Perhaps the cause of the disaster would have remained a mystery forever, but at the court of inquiry into the loss John Rivers' mother confessed that her son had vowed to have revenge on the ship's Captain if it cost him his own life.

That, it seemed, was the end of the schooner *Lady Luvibund*. But, such was not to be the case. For at intervals of fifty years the schooner has been seen racing onto the Goodwins. The first time was on the night of February 13, 1798, when the disaster was observed by very competent witnesses.

On this night Captain James Westlake, in charge of the coasting vessel *Edenbridge* and an excellent and conscientious seaman, was skirting the edge of the Goodwin Sands when he saw a three-masted schooner with all sails set bearing down upon his vessel. Captain Westlake's helmsman saw the schooner also. Indeed it took their united effort to steer aside in time to let this strange craft rush by. And as it passed they distinctly heard sounds of female voices and gaiety coming from the Captain's cabin.

So real was this experience that the moment he went ashore, Captain Westlake reported the near accident to the owners of his ship. He did not dream of saying that he had seen a ghost ship. He was convinced that some Captain had flagrantly disobeyed the rules of the sea and thereby had endangered the safety of the *Edenbridge* and her crew. Captain Westlake was anxious to have the Captain found and punished for what he regarded as criminal carelessness.

The owners of the *Edenbridge* immediately made inquiries, but the only reliable information they uncovered came from the crew of a fishing vessel. They had seen the same schooner go ashore on the Goodwin Sands, where it broke up before their eyes. Nevertheless, when they reached the spot where the vessel had gone down they found nothing but sand and water.

It was fifty years later to the day that the phantom schooner was seen again. This time it was the Deal hovellers—small craftsmen—who sighted the schooner aground on the Goodwin Sands and breaking up rapidly. Launching a boat, they made a very careful search but found nothing. An American clipper which had been passing at the same time agreed with he hovellers that they, too, had seen the vessel. And they all had heard voices and sounds of gaiety as the ship bore down on the sands.

Another fifty years elapsed before the ghost ship was seen again. On this occasion the vessel was sighted by watchers from the shore. Like Captain Westlake, like the hovellers, like the American clipper ship, they saw the schooner pile up on the sands. They launched boat, of course, but a prolonged search failed to reveal any sign of a wreck.

In 1998 there will be many persons looking out at the Goodwin Sands, looking for the ship, *Lady Luvibund*. What is more, the chances are that they will see it, under full sail, smash itself to nothing on the Goodwin Sands.

Amazing Lake Monsters

Lesser-Known Lake Monsters

Dr. Karl P. N. Shuker

September 1990

It is possible that many lakes around the world contain large animal forms unknown to science (at least in the living state). This perennially fascinating subject shows no sign of waning.

To date, however, interest has largely focused on just a small number of cases, e.g., Nessie of Scotland's Loch Ness, Champ of the U.S. Lake Champlain, Ogopogo of Canada's Lake Okanagan, Mokele-Mbembe of the Congo's Lake Tele.

The great majority of other "monster" lakes attract far less public attention. Here, then, is a round-up of recent events from a wide-ranging selection of lesser-known monster lakes.

We begin in North America's Lake Memphremagog, straddling the Quebec-Vermont border, and its monster in residence, Memphre. Thanks to interest in the latter, the study of lake monsters finally received its very own name.

Since 1978, former insurance broker Jacques Boisvert from Magog, Quebec, has been collecting reports of Memphre, some dating back to the early nineteenth century. By the middle of 1988, he had made well over 2,000 scuba-diving forays of this thirty-two-mile-long lake in search of its alleged inhabitant.

One of Boisvert's friends, a monk at the St. Benoit du Lac Benedictine Abbey on Lake Memphremagog's shores, suggested that in view of the nature of his new occupation, Boisvert should call himself a dracontologist—literally, a dragon studier! With that, the study of lake monsters gained an official title: dracontology.

In June 1986, Boisvert and Barbara Malloy—a lady from Newport, Vermont, with a similar interest in Memphre—formed the International Society of Dracontology of Lake Memphremagog, and a few months later the subject received major front-page coverage in the *Boston Globe.*

In addition, as reported in the ISC Newsletter for Summer 1987, the Memphre movement subsequently gathered sufficient momentum for Vermont legislators to adopt on March 17, 1987, a joint resolution by the Senate and House of Representatives, requesting serious scientific investigation, and formal protection of the Lake Memphremagog monster.

What Is a Memphre?

But what of Memphre itself? What does this mystery beast (or beasts) look like? According to reports gathered by Boisvert that involved clear sightings, it resembles a long-necked, dragon-headed creature that moves at a steady pace through the water, almost as if propelled rnechanically. Other accounts merely describe a Nessie-type hump.

In an interview published by Montreal's *Gazette* on August 27, 1988, Boisvert recalled that the world-famous German scuba diver Max Leubker searched the lake back in 1935. He had been hired by a wealthy family to locate the body of one of its members, which had never resurfaced after the person in question had drowned there earlier that year. Despite descending more than 200 feet into the lake (a depth that few divers attain), Leubker never discovered the body. He did report seeing some large eels, "six to eight feet long and as thick as a man's thigh . . . " creatures that not even Boisvert himself has seen during his own dives in more recent years.

Canadian Monster—Mammal or Snake?

Another elongate, Canadian monster may inhabit Lake Shuswap, in central British Columbia. While sailing on the lake on June 3, 1984, Linda Griffiths observed a patch of water 300 feet away which began to churn violently. Focusing on the area with binoculars, she perceived seven bump-like objects, grayish brown in color, visible above the water surface and moving in a straight line at a rapid pace. Mrs. Griffiths believed that it was a fast-moving snake, between twenty to twenty-five feet long.

Her two children (aged twelve and fifteen) and a friend of theirs (thirteen) also saw it, and without binoculars, but none could distinguish any definite head. It crossed in front of the boat before finally submerging (*ISC Newsletter*, Spring 1986). It is unlikely to have been a snake, as these normally swim via lateral undulations rather than vertical ones, but mammals and eels can create vertical disturbances.

Monster Salmon in China

A Chinese lake that has attracted much interest recently is Lake Hanas, a narrow, remote body of water approximately fifteen miles long, with an average depth of roughly 500 feet, and situated in this country's Xinjiang Autonomous Region.

For several decades, villagers in the area have claimed that the lake was inhabited by monsters or big fish, but such creatures did not come to the attention of science until 1985.

As documented in a *China Reconstructs* article (April 1986), in July of that year Xinjiang University biology professor Xiang Lihao and a party of students visited the lake to investigate the area's potential as a wildlife sanctuary. On July 24, they saw several huge, red-colored, boat-like objects moving through the profuse algae at the water's surface.

Using binoculars, the students determined that these objects were enormous fish, estimated at around thirty feet in length. They resembled the huchen (Hucho taimen), the largest species of salmon previously known and an inhabitant of northern Chinese rivers, not normally exceeding six and one half feet.

The view of these mighty creatures was so clear that Prof. Xiang could discern their heads (up to three feet across), tail fins, and spiny dorsal rays. The following day he took many color photos of them. Because one specimen was positioned near two lakeside trees, its distance could be measured, and the fish's length could then be accurately ascertained. It was found to be approximately thirty-three feet, confirming the previous day's estimate.

Two days later, they attempted to catch one of these formidable fishes, using sheep legs as bait, and then wild ducks, but they did not succeed in luring a specimen.

To date, the monster salmon of Lake Hanas have eluded capture, but their existence cannot be denied. Furthermore, measuring more than twice the length of the largest confirmed specimen of freshwater fish on record—a fifteen foot European catfish *Siluris glanis* caught in the 1850s in Belorussia's Dneiper River and probably weighing as much as a ton—their scientific importance cannot be underestimated.

In 1988, an investigation of such creatures via aerial reconnaisance was launched using hovercrafts after fishermen reported seeing three thirteen-foot-long specimens in July (*Detroit News*, August 10, 1988).

Tibetan Lake Monster Terrorizes Locals

A few years before the Lake Hanas revelations, another remote lake had attracted dracontological attention, though on that occasion the mystery of whether it did possess a bona fide mystery species was not ever resolved. Lake Wenbu (sometimes spelled "Wembo") is a fish-rich Tibetan lake, with a depth of about 300 feet and a surface area of about 310 square miles.

In June 1980, the *Peking Evening News* carried a report detailing a number of strange accounts concerning a huge dinosaur or plesiosaur-like monster supposedly inhabiting the lake and terrorizing the nearby villages and local yak herdsmen. In one account, three such eyewitnesses reported a creature of this type surface in the lake, revealing a long neck terminating in a relatively large head, and an enormous body as large as a house.

Another account referred to a yak, left to graze on the lake's shores by a district secretary of the Communist Party. When the secretary returned to collect the yak and take it to market, he was unable to find it, but traces left behind suggested that the hapless creature had been dragged into the lake and devoured there by some other, much larger beast. Most gruesome of all was a report concerning the disappearance of a farmer while rowing on the lake. Locals firmly believed that he had been dragged down into its depths by the monster.

If You Can't Identify It, Shoot It!

Western dracontologists had scarcely assimilated such reports as these before the *Peking Evening News* provided details of yet another Oriental oddity. This report was from Northern China's Lake Tian Chai, ensconced within the crater of Jilin Province's volcano Baitoushan.

In August 1980, a party of meteorological workers and other visitors to the lake reported seeing a huge creature with a body larger than that of a cow, with a cow- or dog-shaped head, a long neck measuring more than three feet, and a flat, duck-like beak (perhaps comparable to the famous duck-billed dinosaurs or hadrosaurs?). Piao Longzhi, one of the meteorologists, actually took a shot at the beast but succeeded only in grazing the top of its head. Understandably, the animal swiftly dove for cover into the lake!

Where Do the Monsters Come From?

It later transpired that such a beast had been sighted a number of times previously, and on one occasion it had been joined by four others. Even if these reports are authentic, and such creatures do exist there, one very significant question (even more telling than that of their zoological identity) still awaits a satisfactory answer. Where have they come from?

Unlike most lake monsters, they could not have lived and bred here for generations, because a volcano erupted as recently as 1702. Any inhabitants of the lake must therefore have entered it sometime after that date.

Just to demonstrate that China does not have the monopoly on Asian lake monsters, other striking forms have been reported from lakes elsewhere in this mysterious continent. For example, in *The Leviathans* (1966) Tim Dinsdale documented the macabre snake-like creatures reported from Malaysia's Tasek Bera in Pahang. In western Java, the eighteen- foot-long turtle- or fish-like monster said to inhabit Lake Patenggang is treated with great reverence by the local fishermen, who burn opium to keep it pacified (*London Times*, February 7, 1977).

Toad-like Beasts Terrify Chinese Scientists

Before moving westward out of Asia, one further Sinian lake monster is included, if only because of the bizarre events surrounding its recent scientific debut. During the summer of 1987, a team of scientists from Peking University, led by biology professor Chen Mok Chun, traveled to some deep freshwater pools near Wuhnan, Hubei Province, in order to film the area and its wildlife. While setting up their television cameras, they were treated to an exhibition of local wildlife far beyond anything that even their wildest imaginations could have conceived.

In full view of the nine scientists, three huge creatures rose out of the pools and moved toward them. Their stunned eyewitnesses likened them to giant toad-like beasts, with grayish white skins, mouths that were six feet across, and eyes larger than rice bowls.

According to Professor Chen, these grotesque creatures silently watched the scientists for a short time. One of the creatures opened its mouth and extended an enormously long tongue, which it wrapped around the cameras on tripods. While it promptly engulfed the tripods, its two companions let forth some eldritch screams, and then all three creatures submerged, disappearing from view.

The delayed-shock reaction experienced by the scientists was so great that one of them dropped to his knees and was physically sick, according to Chinese reports, summarized in various overseas accounts, including a report in a U.S. newspaper *The Examiner* for August 11, 1987.

This incident seems so utterly incredible that one would surely feel justified in dismissing it as a hoax if it were not for the fact that the eyewitnesses in question were all trained scientists, including a major name in Chinese biological research, and all from the country's leading university. In many respects the episode is reminiscent of the current giant frog reports from the vicinity of Ohio's Little Miami River.

The native Indians inhabiting various tropical valleys in South America's Andes frequently report the existence there of a greatly feared, giant form of toad called the *sapo de loma* (toad of the hills), said to be deadly poisonous and capable of preying upon creatures as large as medium-sized birds and rodents.

Science has yet to examine a *sapo de loma*, but it must be remembered that the world's largest species of toad, the Colombian giant toad *Bufo blombergi*, was first made known to science as recently as 1951. Perhaps even larger species still exist in remote regions of the world.

Russia Has Its Monster, Too

The Soviet Union's answer to Nessie and Champ is the monster of Lake Kok-Kol, situated in the Dzambul area of Kazakhstan. Said to have a body measuring up to fifty feet in total length, and a head exceeding six feet, it had attracted considerable interest from Soviet scientists during the 1970s and early 1980s. By 1986, however, expeditions in search of it had come up with an identity that rejected any lake monster considerations. One of the creature's most distinctive attributes was its frequently reported trumpeting call.

As recorded in a January 1986 report by the Soviet news agency Tass and subsequently in Western newspapers, after studying the findings of the expeditions a team from the eminent Soviet Academy of Sciences declared that these sounds were nothing more than the noises produced by air being sucked into cracks connecting the deep lake with underwater cavities, and in which large whirlpools appear that explain reports of turbulence in the lake, hitherto attributed to monsters.

Moving farther west, we come to one of the most unlikely homes for a water monster, the artificial (and hence very recent) Lake Zeegrzynski, eighteen miles north of Poland's capital, Warsaw. In 1982 a bather in the lake was startled by a huge, slimy black head bearing what seemed to him to be rabbit-like ears which suddenly surfaced near him. In a recent survey of lake monsters from Continental Europe (*Fortean Times*, Spring 1986), West German cryptozoologist Ulrich Magin suggested that those "ears" could have been the barbels of a giant catfish, and the monster's estimated length of twenty feet an exaggeration. This identification allies it with comparable creatures reported from as far afield as Africa's Lake Victoria and Upper Nile swamps, South America's Paraguayan Chaco, and West Germany's Lake Zwischenahn.

Northward into Scandinavia brings us to Sweden and the home of the famous Lake Storsjon monster. Less familiar, however, are the monsters allegedly inhabiting Iceland's Lake Kleifarvatn, twenty miles south of the country's capital, Reykjavik. In November 1984, bird hunters Olafur Olafsson and Julius Asgeirsson saw what they assumed to be two rocks lying on the lake's shore. When they drew nearer, however, the "rocks" moved, revealing themselves to be a pair of huge animals that began to cavort on the beach.

Olaffson and Asgeirsson observed them from a distance of only a few hundred yards, and described them as being larger than horses, and moving in a dog-like manner on land, but when they entered the water they swam like seals. According to a *Nessletter* report (June 1985), these remarkable animals left behind some distinct but most unusual footprints on the beach, which resembled those of a cow, but had three rather than two toe impressions, and in overall size were larger than those of a horse. Worth mentioning here, as noted by J. Simpson in *Icelandic Folktales and Legends* (1972), is that Icelanders believe in a mythical lake monster called the *nykur* or *nennir*, whose description as a horse-like water beast and wild behavior compare closely with the kelpie or water-horse lore of Scotland.

The British Isles is the last port of call for this article. We journey to the shores of Lake Bala, in Wales. This is the lake that hosted a sighting in 1983 by one of the town's inhabitants of an object about ten feet in length, moving slowly toward the bank. As Chris Barber reported in More Mysterious Wales (1986), its eyewitness was astonished, and rushed after it, but it had vanished. Such a sighting is far from unique here. Over the past twenty years or so a monster has been reported many times in the lake, known locally as Anghenfil or Teggy.

On one occasion it was sighted by Bala's own greengrocer, John Rowlands, who described it as being about eight feet long with dark shiny skin, and a large head that possessed staring eyes. As noted by Janet and Colin Bord in *Ancient Mysteries of Britain* (1986), Rowlands wondered if it could have been a seal left over from the submarine detection training program that took place in the lake during World War I which used live seals. In contrast, the lake's warden, Dewi Bowen, who has also caught sight of something odd here, said that the creature which he saw looked more like a crocodile.

Will the Lake Monster Riddle Ever Be Solved?

Recent lake monster activity is by no means confined to just a few well-publicized lakes, nor does it merely involve a single type of creature. The discoveries made at Lakes Seattle and Washington, not to mention China's Lake Hanas, offer hope to dracontologists everywhere that one day the really famous lake monster mysteries will also be solved, with Nessie, Champ, and the rest finally acquiring an unequivocal place in the annals of zoology, formally named and listed in the catalogue of creatures whose existence on Earth is no longer in doubt.

Are They the Same?

Jon Erik Beckjord

May 1990

The last head to appear is the most bizarre, and the hardest to accept.

The names run off the tongue, with similarities between some of them. Could it be that the creatures also are similar? I would suggest that the answer is yes, and for many reasons.

I am fortunate to have a huge number of photos, drawings, and descriptions of these creatures. Since not everyone knows these names, let me explain that Nessie inhabits Loch Ness and is the best-known lake monster. Chessie hails from the Chesapeake Bay region of Maryland, and Tessie is found in Lake Tahoe, on the California/Nevada line.

Mokele M'bembe guards small (three miles long) Lac Telle in the Republic of the Congo (a place that will eat up an investigator's money), Ogopogo wiggles around Lake Okanangan in British Columbia, and Champ is the queen of Lake Champlain, which crosses Vermont and Canada. All are alleged lake monsters, all have differences, and all have some similarities. For a detailed background of each, see the bibliography in the book by Henry Bauer, *The Enigma of Loch Ness*.

Differences and Similarities

What, then, are these differences and similarities? Nessie has been sighted and filmed in many shapes, but most often in two basic forms: a plesiosaur shape and a serpentine shape. Chessie seems to be mostly a serpentine shape, according to Mike Frizzell, of the Enigma Project in Reisterstown, Maryland.

Tessie is rarely seen, and was filmed just once in a roll of film that the local chamber of commerce, who owns the film, will not allow to be viewed, lest it scare away tourists. In the film and descriptions by witnesses, it is also a long object that never shows a head, flipper, or fin.

Ogopogo has been described mostly as a serpentine shape, recently with a fluked tail by one witness; with no tail flukes by most others. Occasionally a humped back is reported.

Champ is mostly seen as a serpentine object, like a telephone pole that moves, except with undulations. Two visual aids, however, show something else. The Mansi photo shows a humped back with a long neck and a head, and the Hall video shows a hump with a neck as well. Yet, a number of photos taken by Ms. Kelly Williams shows another serpentine telephone pole.

Mokele M'bembe is special and will be discussed below.

Although some of the descriptions and photos of the same (or different) creatures are similar or identical, some are wildly different. A researcher must ask, "How can we reconcile all these differences?"

A Solution in a New Theory

If we stick to the old idea that these creatures are animals, we are caught in a dead end, for no animal, or animals, could account for all these variations that seem at times incompatible. It is simply too much to expect that a basilosaurus (an ancient whale), a plesiosaur, a giant snake, and a monster worm could all exist side by side in these different lakes. Michael Meurger has written a book called *Monsters of Canadian Lakes*, and in it he points out that different lakes have different-looking lake monsters, and other lakes have several different kinds of lake monsters. It is hard enough to accept one basic monster without having to accept the idea of several different kinds, all coexisting in different lakes.

As a solution, I offer a new version of an older idea about Nessie and those of like ilk. Ted Holiday (see his book *The Goblin Universe*) and others in the past have suggested that Nessie may have come from, and gone back to, some other dimension, and may not be a normal animal at all. This concept is very difficult to prove and is beyond our current scientific ability to test. Most researchers feel that Holiday's ideas are too far out.

However, if we rephrase these ideas into a more testable hypothesis, the results may explain the similarities of Nessie, Chessie, etc., as well as the differences. At the same time, it may bring about a focus on the lake phenomenon problem. The zoological path has proven to be a dead end.

Let us look at Nessie, Chessie, etc., as an energy phenomenon that can change to solid matter for short periods of time—

perhaps even energy phenomena that has either guidance or intelligence, or an ability to react to the expectations and/or knowledge of their observers. An energy form might take the shape of a moving energized streak in the water. If it is able to feed off the expectations of its observers, it could take a more definite form as it moves along. Perhaps in lakes where there are no viewers the phenomenon might not take any form at all.

A good example is Lake Tahoe and Tessie. Few people expect a lake monster to appear in high and remote Lake Tahoe. Few lake monster experts visit there. Thus, the phenomenon asserts itself as a long, narrow body with no head and no tail. Perhaps if researchers were to live there, future sightings might feature a head, hump, and tail.

Miss Alexandria David-Neel, a French scholar and traveler, has written in her book, *Magic and Mystery of Tibet*, of the idea of forming "tulpoids" or creatures made from mental constructs, "mind creatures." If it is true that the mind can form physical or semi-physical beings, then maybe the lake monsters are given much of their form from the thoughts, conscious or otherwise, of the observers.

A Recent Example

I was at Loch Ness in 1983, the fiftieth anniversary of Loch Ness research, trying to use robot video to catch the image of Nessie. Our results were marginal with this technique. One day while waiting for a TV program to air about our efforts, I observed a series of rings being formed in the water about mile away. Fish do this, but these rings caught my attention because they were being formed in a straight line, one ring after another, some ten feet apart.

I watched with ten power binoculars, and saw, I thought, two small, straw-shaped objects, less than two inches long, surfacing to form each ring, then submerging. I waited, tried to film them with a telephoto lens, and watched some more. At one point I thought I saw a pink body, perhaps six feet long, almost surface, and then submerge. It had neither fins, head, nor tail that I could see. The body slightly reminded me of a Florida manatee. The film did not turn out, and I resolved to watch for this again the next time the water was calm.

Later, on one of the last days spent at the Loch, we had gotten up early from a caravan at Achnahannet, some miles away from the Clansmen Hotel where the first ring-sightings had occurred. At 8:00 A.M., I noticed the same sort of rings forming, this time going toward Fort Agustus to our right. I pulled out a movie camera and proceeded to shoot the rings as they formed, perhaps at three mph, going down the Loch in the calm water. As I filmed with three people watching, I wondered if it would surface. I had to stop twice to wind the film, and as the film ran out, the rings subsided and petered out.

I thought nothing much would come of the film, and paid little attention to it until I returned to the U.S. However, after a number of viewings, it gradually became apparent that more than a series of rings had been filmed. What appeared at first to be a mere water disturbance became a progression of form on the water rather than in it. The white rings expanded to form a long streak. The streak undulated, like a pair of linked inchworms, and these in turn became a comet-like form, taking on a shape similar to a Concorde jet, on the calm, blue water.

To my surprise, enlargements showed a gray rounded face, sometimes with two horns mounted above, looking at the four of us around the camera. To do this, the thing had to crank its head over at a ninety-degree angle, looking sideways and up, while still moving forward. Dr. Maccabee agrees that there is a triangular nose, and other views see a set of eyes, and a mouth with some heavy duty teeth—like a set of short walrus tusks—

mounted aiming downward. The face image has little contrast, which is typical of energy phenomena of a less controversial type, such as moving mist, or windstorm. Overall, it seems a cross between a cat, an otter, and a walrus. It was found to measure ten feet, so otters are out, cats are out, and there are no ten-foot white walruses in Loch Ness. Los Angeles zoologists agree that it is nothing known to them.

Each frame of the film shows a changed form and a changed face. Further in the film the object changes again to a linear water disturbance, a frothy line on the surface. After I had wound the camera, the object changed again and continued to change.

The last head to appear is the most bizarre, and the hardest to accept. In six frames, up comes a white blob, unformed, and in under one second the head took on definite features. It looks like a man's head, bald, with two tufts of hair, somewhat rectangular, rounded in shape, with wide open eyes, a nose, and a mouth. In two more seconds, it has gone down under the water, and at that point the film stops, needing to be wound again. The last sequence shows just an occasional ring in the water, then nothing. The water is calm, as if nothing had happened.

Dr. Maccabee agrees that the object moves, and is probably animate, and that it looked at us. Zoologists at the Los Angeles Museum of Natural History agree that the film shows no known animal or fish. Other zoologists discount even a school of small fish. Operation Deepscan, a sonar effort at Loch Ness in October 1987, discovered that schools of bait fish do exist, but at least fifty feet down and not on the surface. Thus, the object seems to be the Loch Ness phenomenon, or Nessie.

My point in this analysis is to show that it may be possible that our own thoughts affected the image that the phenomenon radiated to our camera. As it progressed to our right, it may have grown in substance due to input from our collective thoughts about what Nessie should be like. As it got beyond range, it subsided to nothing. It starts as almost nothing, grows to a ten-foot object, becomes a series of appearing and disappearing heads, then subsides to nothing—something like a bell curve in intensity Of note might be that the John Cobb Memorial was one mile away, and Cobb, a racer, died in a jet boat in 1952 at that spot. Cobb was bald, and had thin hair on the sides of his face.

Perhaps Nessie, Tessie, Chessie and the others have been affected by the preconceptions, or lack of same, of lakeside viewers. The very strongest images with the most detail—heads, humps, tails, tails with spikes, and backs with triangular stegosaurus-type projections are found in Loch Ness, which draws a very literate and educated group of visitors. Nobody expects a Tessie, or a Chessie, so their images are less complex. Champ has almost as much press as Nessie, and thus its image is often complex. Ogopogo is felt by many people to be so far from Loch Ness that any similarity is remote, so its image, fed from the minds of visitors, is more Chessie-like.

The Mystery of Mokele M'bembe

Mokele M'bembe is the dollar drainer of the African continent. Herman Regusters, who saw the creature in 1981, has made a hump-and-neck type drawing that brings to mind Nessie. Zoo director Marcellin Agagna has done the same. Colonel E. Mossedzedi of the Congo army has drawn a very worm-like rendering of MM, based on his own sighting of the creature. It looks more like a large worm or snake than like any brontosaurus, or even plesiosaur.

In the 1970s, explorer James Powell asked natives about the creature and showed them photos of animals like hippos and elephants, with other photos of re-creations of prehistoric animals mixed in. Invariably, the natives picked either the brontosaurus or the plesiosaur.

These images may have reinforced a tulpoid Mokele M'bembe's shape. Where the earliest pygmies and other local natives got their mental images from, we do not know. In any case, there are more reports of MM being of the plesiosaur form than the snake form, and thus it tends to be different from the Northern Hemisphere lake monsters. The mechanics of its mental-energy feeding process, however, appear to be the same, with the same result. Mokele M'bembe seems to be more in the lake monster mold than the dinosaur mold, and it is most often encountered in the water, over its head—not the usual habitat for a brontosaurus.

There do exist stories of sea serpents in the Southern Hemisphere, and while these are not lake monsters, I will throw in a brief account of a sea serpent seen by a hotel manager from Mamatanai, New Ireland, Papua New Guinea, while I was there in 1983, debunking stories of natives eating mermaids. It seems that twice In the 1970s this manager, an Englishman, had encountered a fifty foot serpent lying underwater on the sea bottom in a lagoon near Ramat Bay. He described it as looking like Chessie: a large, snake-like thing, and he avoided disturbing it lest it decide to eat him for lunch. Ramat Bay was where many of the alleged mermaids were seen, which later were proven to be dugongs, a relative of the manatee.

Intelligent Energy?

Perhaps the same energy phenomenon is in all the lakes of the world, and it reflects to viewers what their background, racial memories, education, and expectations send to the phenomenon. The more sophisticated the viewers, the more likely the image received is equally sophisticated. However, this may not be completely true in all instances. The images seen are too varied to be of mere animals, and a better theory, which physics can someday test, is a theory of intelligent energy, reflecting our own thoughts and images to us.

I propose that Nessie, Chessie, Tessie, Ogopogo, and Champ are all the same phenomenon. So too is Mokele M'bembe, but with some regional and perhaps foreigner-influenced input that results in it seeming to be of the hump and neck type.

If the alleged lake monsters are viewed as being unknown energy phenomena, all the apparent contradictions fall away and the path is cleared for physics to make sense of something where zoology could not.

America's Water Monsters: The New Evidence

Jerome Clark

April 1983

The woman stared in astonishment as a creature from a prehistoric age rose from beneath the water.

The first known sighting of an unusual animal in Lake Champlain was made, appropriately enough, by that lake's namesake, the great French explorer Samuel de Champlain, who reported seeing something "serpent like" and "about twenty feet long and as thick as a barrel, with a head that resembled that of a horse." That was in 1609. In following centuries numerous other people have said they too saw a mysterious creature in the enormous lake.

Lake Champlain is over 100 miles long and thirteen miles across at its widest point. Covering 436 square miles along the borders of New York, Vermont, and Quebec, it has an average depth of sixty-four feet, and some spots are up to 400 feet deep. It is the largest North American lake not classified as one of the Great Lakes. It has more than enough room, some people say, to house a whole family of monsters.

Believing a creature like "Champ" (as the monster has come to be called) exists and proving that it actually does are, of course, two different matters. The 170 reports Champ investigator Joseph Zarzynski has collected are more or less consistent in their descriptions, but skeptics have argued that eyewitness reports are not enough since even sincere, well-meaning people can be fooled into thinking a log, an otter, or a diving bird is a large animal unknown to science. Such arguments have long been used to discredit sightings of alleged lake monsters elsewhere in the world. As a result the debate over the reality of the creatures was stalemated long ago.

But this may be about to change, thanks to a series of events that began in early July 1977, when Anthony and Sandra Mansi of Groton, Connecticut, were vacationing in Vermont. They had driven past Saint Albans Bay in the the west corner of the state and were somewhere near the Canadian border when they decided to stop and let their small children play in the water.

They parked their car and walked 100 to 200 feet across a field, then descended a six-foot bank to the waterline. As the children waded near the shore, Mansi went back to the car to retrieve his glasses and a camera. Some moments later Mrs. Mansi noticed bubbles in the water about 150 feet away. She thought a diver was about to surface. She was wrong. She found herself gaping in astonishment at a huge animal with a small head, long neck, and humped back. It looked like a monster from a prehistoric age. The creature was moving its head right and left.

By this time Anthony Mansi had returned and he too watched the thing with mounting alarm. "Let's get out of here!" he shouted. He and Sandra called the children (who, unaware of what was happening in the water behind them, never saw the creature) and Anthony tossed the camera to Sandra. "Take a picture!" he suggested. She shot one picture before the animal sank—it did not dive—under the water. The sighting had lasted between two and four minutes. The Mansis had the picture developed and were pleased to see how well it turned out. But fearing ridicule, they were reluctant to show it to anyone. They put it in a family album and misplaced the negative. Eventually Mrs. Mansi confided the story to friends at work and showed them the photograph. Duly impressed, these friends started telling other people and by 1980 the story got to Zarzynski, an upstate New York social studies teacher who has spent most of his adult life investigating reports of unknown animals in Lake Champlain. Zarzynski contacted the Mansis and got them to cooperate in a study of what seemed a remarkable piece of scientific evidence for Champ's existence.

Zarzynski sought the opinions of scientists who might be able to identify the "object" (the neutral term investigators would use) in the photograph. Vermont state naturalist Charles Johnson declared it resembled no known animal in the lake. George Zug, Chairman of the Department of Vertebrate Zoology at the Smithsonian Institution's National Museum of Natural History, said it resembled no known animal anywhere. But biologist Roy Mackal noted its similarity to the world's most celebrated unknown animal—the Loch Ness monster.

Dr. Mackal is the vice president of the National Society of Cryptozoology, formed in January 1982 when a group of biologists and paleontologists met at the Smithsonian to discuss ways to investigate persistent reports of "hidden" animals such as lake monsters, sea serpents, and Bigfoot, which have been the subject of popular speculation but little scientific inquiry.

Mackal sent the photograph to ISC secretary J. Richard Greenwell, who was employed at the University of Arizona. Greenwell and D. Roy Frieden of the university's Optical Sciences Center began a careful analysis of the picture. Dr. Frieden determined that the photograph was not a montage; in other words, it had not been doctored by someone pasting the image of Champ over a photograph of the lake. Furthermore, he concluded, the wave patterns around the object purporting to be Champ suggested vertical rather than horizontal disturbance, which meant that the "object" had come up from under the surface instead of moving along the surface as would be the case if it were an artificial device being pulled by a rope.

But Frieden and Greenwell were not about to jump to conclusions. They took the picture to nearby Kitt Peak National Observatory and had a black-and-white transparency made from the color print. Using a sophisticated image-enhancement technique, the scientists were able to obtain an extraordinarily detailed view of the image. Unfortunately they still could not see any features on the object's head, which was heavily in shadow. They found no evidence of a hoax but at the same time they could not establish that the object was a living animal.

Frieden was troubled by the presence of a brownish streak in the original print. Maybe it was a sandbar, he suggested. And if it was, maybe the picture was a hoax—the hoaxer could have waded out from shore and launched a monster model from the sandbar. Mackal, on the other hand, took a more positive view. He pointed out that witnesses to the Loch Ness monster frequently have reported seeing it as it waded in shallow water, perhaps waiting for fish runs.

How big was the object? That is the question. A large size would lessen the likelihood of a hoax, because a huge model would be difficult and expensive to construct, transport, and float. (If that were the case, then the Mansis would have to be the perpetrators, not the victims, of a hoax because they firmly insist that the thing they saw looked and acted like an animal.)

The photograph, unfortunately, provides no clear points of reference. It does not, for example, show precisely where the shoreline begins, which would have helped investigators determine the dimensions of the object and its distance from the observers. The distance of the object from the photographer was a major issue. After all, something that appeared that large from a distance of fifty feet would have to be of pretty respectable proportions. But the information needed to resolve this question simply wasn't immediately available.

There was another method of determining the object's approximate size: the length of the waves around it. University of British Columbia oceanographer Paul H. LeBlond, a leading authority on waves and another member of ISC's Board of Directors, agreed to conduct the analysis. In his report, released in the fall of 1982, Dr. LeBlond explains, "The appearance of the sea surface is often described in terms of the characteristics of the waves. A scale which relates wave properties to wind speed is the familiar Beaufort scale, which assigns a Beaufort number and a range of wind speeds to different sea states. The conditions corresponding to Beaufort Number 3, for a range of wind speeds between seven and twelve miles per hour, consist of 'large wavelets, crests begin to break; scattered whitecaps.' These are the conditions observed on the Mansi photograph."

Using a formula that relates the speed of the wind and the distance of the open water over which the wind blows to wave properties, LeBlond estimated the waves to be between sixteen and thirty-nine feet in length. When he compared the "unknown object" (Champ) with the waves in its vicinity, he discovered that it occupied one-and-a-half to two wavelengths. Therefore, he concluded, the part of the object that was above water could not be less than twenty-four feet or more than seventy-eight feet long. In short, the object was enormous.

While it is impossible to prove that the Mansi photograph is not a hoax, so far there is no reason to believe it is a hoax and considerable reason to believe it is not. If the object was a model we would expect it to be relatively small and we would expect its motion on the water to be that of a device being pulled by a rope; in other words, it would be moving horizontally across the lake surface. Instead, as we would expect if we were dealing with a genuine aquatic animal, the Mansi photograph shows a huge object that has risen from under the water. If this is a hoax, the hoaxers—presumably the Mansis—went to a great deal of trouble and expended a sizeable amount of cash to pull it off. (LeBlond's analysis, by the way, revealed that the "brownish streak" was probably a reflection on the water; it was definitely not a sandbar, as Frieden had theorized when he suggested that perhaps hoaxers had launched a monster model from one.)

If Sandra Mansi did help perpetrate a difficult, expensive hoax, why did she take only one photograph? And why did she hide it for well over three years before allowing investigators to examine it?

The scientists who are studying the picture are working on the assumption that it is what it seems to be: a strikingly clear color photograph of America's best-known lake monster. Even the most skeptical scientist participating in the investigation, biologist Forrest Wood of the U.S. Navy's Naval Ocean Systems Center, now believes the picture depicts a large unknown animal.

What kind of animal is Champ? Because so little is known about it, theories are in short supply. The only firm conclusion investigators have come to is that, whatever Champ is, it is probably the same kind of beast witnesses have reported at Loch Ness in Scotland, at Lake Okanagan in Canada, and at numerous other lakes around the world. Roy Mackal is convinced the animals are zeuglodons, primitive serpentlike whales that supposedly have been extinct for twenty million years. Others, such as J. Richard Greenwell, take a more radical view: that the creatures may be aquatic dinosaurs of the plesiosaur type.

But these are just speculations and they will remain nothing more until scientists have a body, not just a picture, at their disposal. But would-be fortune hunters who think of going to Lake Champlain to bag Champ with a harpoon or high-powered rifle should be aware that since November 1980 the Port Henry, New York, city council has made it illegal to "harm or harass" Champ in the waters of Bulwagga Bay, the area of the lake that borders the town from the east. And in April 1982 the Vermont House of Representatives passed a resolution urging that Champ "be protected from any willful act resulting in death, injury, or harassment."

Meanwhile sightings of the creature continue. In May 1982 six bowlers from Moriah, New York, reported seeing a twenty-five-foot-long animal with reptilian humps on its back. On July 19 Claude Van Kleeck, camping with friends on a beach at Port Henry, saw a "blackish gray" object in the water. "As thick as an oil drum," it appeared to be about fifty feet long. When it got within 300 feet of shore, Van Kleeck snapped a picture of it with an expensive 35mm camera with a telephoto lens. Unfortunately the photograph developed blank because the film failed to advance inside the camera.

Move Over, Champ

If Champ has become America's most famous lake monster, Chessie—the Chesapeake Bay monster—may be about to offer some serious competition for the title. In early July 1982 a reported sighting of the creature received widespread attention in newspapers and on television network news broadcasts. The cause of the exitement was the fact that one of the witnesses had videotaped the creature's appearance. At 7:00 P.M. on May 31, 1982, Robert and Karen Frew were entertaining guests outside their home which overlooks the bay at Love Point, at the mouth of the Chester River. Love Point, at the northern tip of Kent Island, is across the bay from Annapolis, Maryland.

When first spotted, the creature was about 200 feet from shore, in calm, shallow water about five feet deep. Frew watched it through binoculars for a few minutes before securing his video camera and focusing on the mysterious animal, which submerged and reappeared several times during the sighting. The closest the creature came was within 100 feet of shore and within fifty feet of some boys who were playing on a pile of submerged rocks. Although the Frews and their guests shouted to alert the boys (their cries and all other com- ments made during the event are recorded on the videotape), the boys never heard them and so (like the Mansi children) never saw the animal. Frew thinks it is just as well. "If they'd seen it at eye level," he says, "there would have been mass panic." Witnesses estimated the animal to be thirty to thirty-five feet long but slightly less than a foot in diameter. Much of it remained under water, but as it surfaced repeatedly, more and more of it became visible. Frew says, "The first time up, we saw its head and about four feet [of back]. The next time about twelve feet, the next time about twenty." The visible part of the back seemed to have humps. Its head was shaped like a football, only "a little more round." Observers could not make out features such as eyes, ears, or a mouth. It was the odd shape of the head more than anything else that led Frew to reject the idea that the animal was some kind of snake.

In fact, the thing didn't look like anything the Frews had ever seen before and they had observed a variety of animals, including sea turtles, sharks, and otters, in the bay. But this was something else.

On August 20, 1982, seven scientists from the Smithsonian, along with representatives of the National Aquarium and Maryland's Department of Natural Resources, met at the Smithsonian to view and discuss the Frew videotape. In a subsequent report describing the group's conclusions, zoologist George Zug wrote, "All the viewers of the tape came away with a strong impression of an animate object . . . . We could not identify the object . . . . These sightings are not isolated phenomena, for they have been reported regularly for the past several years." Among the other sightings was one made in 1981 by a Mrs. Pennington, who took 35mm color photographs of unknown animal or animals she saw while taking an early morning walk along the banks of the Choptank River, which flows into Chesapeake Bay from eastern Maryland. She saw, in Zug's words, "three angular objects swimming in a straight line and producing a single strong wake. The shape of [the] angular objects was certainly similar to the 'head' in the Frew videotape; however, Mrs. Pennington believes that the three objects were the above-water parts of a single object. We could neither confirm nor deny this assumption nor were we able to identify the object(s). The distinct and strong wake [in the pictures] does show that the object was moving and moving at a fair rate of speed."

The Frew and Pennington reports are consistent with others made by Chessie witnesses. A more or less typical sighting took place in June 1980, when G. F. Green III and his family saw "some kind of serpent" with "three or four humps." The Greens, who were waterskiing in the bay at the time, said the creature—about twenty-five feet long—was swimming smoothly and rapidly. "Every now and then you'd see the head pop up," Green said. "But when we'd get close to it, it would suddenly sink down and disappear."

Long History of Sightings

Reports of "monsters" in American lakes and rivers go back a long way. The earliest accounts are preserved in Indian legends. European explorers and white settlers in this country also told of seeing large, unidentified aquatic creatures. But few people and even fewer scientists believed them.

Nonetheless the reports continued—and now growing numbers of scientists are paying serious attention to them. The initial investigations of the International Society of Cryptozoology show there is excellent reason to take seriously the proposition that such creatures exist.

The Shy Monster of Loch Ness

Paul Foght

May 1961

"Nessie" may avoid the limelight—but new research techniques are putting the famed what's-it on stage.

Scientists ringed the shores of Scotland's Loch Ness with elaborate sighting and photographic instruments for the 1960 monster-viewing season, but Nessie didn't cooperate.

However, the concerted effort by teams of biologists, zoologists, and photographers did produce three pieces of evidence which have allowed one scientist to construct a hypothetical picture of the world's most famous monster.

The first exhibit is two photographs of wave patterns made by an unseen animal swimming near the surface of

Loch Ness last summer. These pictures, made by a team headed by Maurice Burton, D.Sc., are being studied by experts including naval architects because a body moving through the surface of the water creates a characteristic bow-wave and wake. These disturbances are strong clues to the shape and size of the body that causes them.

The second piece of pro-monster evidence is an old photograph which is given new credence by current expert opinion. In preparing their assualt on the monster's lair, the scientists prepared a detailed study of alleged snapshots of the Loch Ness animal. The most famous of these photos, a shot taken in April 1934, shows the head and long slender neck of the monster, and often has been denounced as a fake. A new photographic analysis of this picture has disclosed faint sets of ripples in the water around the protruding parts of the monster's body. Photo experts reported that fakery of geometry and the "varying degree of wash and counterwash" in the photo would be virtually impossible.

The third and final bit of pro-monster evidence is a statistical survey which the men of science made while they waited for Nessie. Althought first mention of the "fearsome beast" of Loch Ness was made in the sixth century by St. Columba, the first modern sighting of the creature was reported in May 1933. Since that first sighting, 3,000 eyewitness accounts have been recorded.

Analysis of these 3,000 reports showed that the majority of the sightings were in glassy, calm weather. Dr. Burton feels that this fact tends to rule out the skeptical explanation that the monster is an illusion created by shadow or wave action.

Further statistical analysis tends to dispel the popular picture of the monster as a beast with three humps on its back. Dr. Burton's analysis found that one-third of the reports tell of one hump and another one-fourth describe two humps.

The most important statistic, in Dr. Burton's opinion, is that one-third of the reports tell of a long neck with a small head, either alone or in conjunction with one or more humps.

From these three forms of evidence, Dr. Burton has constructed a hypothetical Loch Ness monster. He sees the animal as a vertebrate reptile, fully adapted to an aquatic life, having a body like a long-necked penguin, but probably having two sets of flippers instead of the penguin's single pair. This conformation is not too remote from the body of a prehistoric plesiosaur.

More biologists and more photographers will hit the beaches of Loch Ness for the 1961 season, but Dr. Burton warns that experience in photographing wild animals proves that they'll have to be very lucky to capture a portrait of the Loch Ness tourist magnet.

Rethinking the Loch Ness Monster

Betty Lou White
December 1968

A three-year grant from Field Enterprises helps scientists close in on the loch's troubled waters.

Scotland's Loch Ness—full of peat in suspension and deeper in most places that the North Sea—long has been considered the world's most fitting habitat for a monster. Seven years ago a private scientific organization was formed to search for this monster. Based in London, the Anglo-American Loch Ness Phenomena Investigation Bureau, Ltd., in 1968 came into possession of photographic research equipment, biopsy darts, and related equipment through a three-year grant from Field Enterprises Educational Corp., publishers of *World Book Encyclopedia.*

Chief of the American branch for the Loch Ness investigation is Prof. Roy P. Mackal, University of Chicago biologist. In a research paper based on his findings in the loch in 1967, Professor Mackal speaks of the new evidence which resulted when he employed one of the oldest techniques of police work, the artist's sketch. The biologist and an animal illustrator collaborated in checking the various descriptions of the "monster" against known zoological possibilities.

Professor Mackal theorizes the type of animal that fits most of the descriptive evidence and photos has to be a large aquatic mammal which could live above 50 degrees north latitude (Loch Ness is 57 degrees north).

He found astonishing similarities between the reported appearances and behavior of the monster and those of the northern sea cow, known as long as 200 years ago in the Bering Sea. Now nearly extinct in northern waters, the sea cows are members of an order of sea animals called sirenians, ancestrally related, Mackal says, to elephants.

There's one catch though. The sea cow is herbivorous, while the Loch Ness creature must live on fish. There isn't enough vegetable plankton in the loch to feed even a baby monster. However, Mackal says it is biologically possible for a northern sea cow to have become carnivorous or that a fish-eating branch of the species exists.

Sizing Up Sea Serpents

Sea Serpents Do Exist

Jared Hamilton

November 1950

Even biologists now admit that there must be some gigantic unknown animal in the seas.

On May 22, 1917, the British armed Merchant Cruiser *Hilary*, Captain F. W. Dean, Royal Navy, was cruising southeast of Iceland as a link in the blockade of Germany. Captain Dean was sitting in his cabin writing a letter when the report was shouted down from the bridge: "Object on the starboard quarter."

Captain Dean raced up to the bridge asking if it was a periscope. The watch pointed to an object at some distance which Captain Dean first mistook for a floating tree trunk with the branches lopped off, leaving short stubs. He trained his glasses on the object, however, and soon became convinced that the thing was alive and that what he had thought were knobs were in fact the head and dorsal fins of an unknown marine animal.

It occurred to Captain Dean that this would make a good target for anti-submarine practice, since things were dull on the ship. He manned the six-pounder guns which the *Hilary* carried, but before giving the order to fire he thought it might be a good idea to run up closer to the queer beast and have a look at it.

The *Hilary* changed course and headed toward the unknown creature, passing within thirty yards of it. Captain Dean later described the head as somewhat larger than that of a cow, but of approximately the same shape. The head was smooth and there were no horns or ears visible. It was black except for what appeared to be a white streak between the nostrils. The animal reared its head to look at the ship as it steamed by but it did not seem to be alarmed in any way.

Behind the neck, what Captain Dean took to be a dorsal fin showed about four feet above the water. It was black and apparently thin. There seemed to be no bones in it, as a fish's fin might have, because it flopped over like a fold of skin.

Captain Dean estimated that the neck of the animal was twenty feet between the head and the start of the fin. He estimated the entire length of the creature at sixty feet, assuming that the fin began at the place where the neck and body joined.

The *Hilary* steamed by at twelve knots, not disturbing the fantastic creature in any way. It continued to lie on the surface, undulating in the swells. When they had passed it by 1,200 yards the *Hilary* was turned about and the first guns began to open up on the animal. It was a small target, and each of the three gun crews took their turn, firing five shots at the animal.

The second shot of the third crew hit the creature. It thrashed about violently for a few seconds and then disappeared. The *Hilary* passed over the spot where the animal had been but there was no sign of it.

This strange encounter of the *Hilary* is only one of hundreds of recorded meetings of ships with an unknown marine animal that resembles a giant sea serpent. As we'll see later, the creature is not a serpent, and quite possibly is an animal, but it is unknown to zoologists and its existence is doubted by many of them.

The men who report seeing this unknown denizen of the deep have one characteristic in common—they are all brave. If they were not, they would never dare report seeing such impossible monsters as sea serpents. Such is the disposition of skeptical man that he accepts the most outrageous lies with equanimity, but cannot stomach the truth. In these cases, the captains who reported sea serpents were hooted down and scoffed at.

They were suspected when they sought new berths, for who wants to serve under a man suffering from hallucinations, and who wants to hire such a man? As a result, it is certain that countless sea serpents have been sighted without a report ever being made because the witnesses were afraid of being laughed at. Indeed, there is good evidence to support belief in a general conspiracy of silence on these phenomena.

There is one recorded case in which a captain was dining in his cabin and refused to come to the bridge to witness a sea serpent reported by the mate. He was afraid that if he did see such a phenomenon he would be obliged to report it and might be a laughing stock the rest of his life.

One of the brave was German Captain Freiherr von Forstner, commander of the submarine U-28 during World

War I. On July 30, 1915, the U-28 torpedoed a British merchant ship in the North Atlantic. The ship, the *Iberian*, sank rapidly and exploded at a great depth. Captain von Forstner thought the explosion might have been well over a mile deep, since the Iberian had sunk nearly thirty seconds before the explosion came. Shortly after the explosion, a gigantic sea animal was thrown more than sixty feet into the air. Six crewmen of the U-28 saw the beast and watched it thrashing about on the surface for several seconds before it disappeared. Captain von Forstner said it was over sixty feet long, and looked something like a giant alligator, with four paddles on the side of a large body. It had a long neck, long tail, and pointed head.

One of the widely publicized recent sightings of sea serpents goes back less than three years to December 30, 1947. It was 11:55 A.M. and the Grace Line Steamer *Santa Clara* was proceeding in calm weather under blue skies east of Cape Lookout, en route from New York to Cartagena, Spain.

Third Mate John Axelson suddenly saw a reptilian head rear out of the sea just off the ship's bow. Two other mates then saw it and the three watched it as it came even with the bridge and finally was left astern.

They estimated that the animal's head was about five feet long and about half as thick. The water around the creature was stained red and they assumed that the ship had cut it in two. They saw a long thin snake-like body about thirty-five feet long. Throughout the time they were watching it, the creature was thrashing about, as though it was badly hurt. There was no hair or knobs to be seen, or any fins. Color was dark brown. It could not be verified that the *Santa Clara* actually had cut the monster in two because there were no witnesses on the other side of the ship.

In 1892, a Dutch zoologist, A. C. Oudemans, a member of the Royal Dutch Zoological Society, published a book called *The Great Sea Serpent*, which contains reports of over 200 sightings of sea serpents. A great number of these are considered to be authentic.

The earliest eyewitness account of a sea serpent on record is that of a Norwegian priest, Hans Egede, who reported seeing a strange animal off the west coast of Greenland in 1734. He said the head was raised above his main top. It had a pointed nose and blew like a whale, large broad flippers and a long tail.

Perhaps the most famous encounter with a sea serpent was that of Captain Peter M'Quhae of Her Majesty's Ship *Daedalus* on August 6, 1848. The *Daedalus* was heading back to England from the Indies and had rounded the Cape of Good Hope and was somewhere southeast of St. Helena. Here are excerpts from a letter M'Quhae wrote to the Admiralty on official stationery:

> On our attention being called to the object it was discovered to be an enormous serpent, with head and shoulders kept about four feet constantly above the surface of the sea, and as nearly as we could approximate by comparing it with the length of what our main topsail yard should show in the water, there was at the very least sixty feet of the animal in the water, no portion of which was, to our perception, used in propelling it through the water, either by vertical or horizontal undulation. It passed rapidly, but so close under our lee quarter that had it been a man of my acquaintance I should have easily recognized his features with the naked eye; and it did not, either in approaching the ship or after it had passed our wake, deviate in the slightest degree from its course to the southwest, which it held on at a constant pace of from twelve to fifteen knots, apparently on some determined purpose.

> The diameter of the serpent was about fifteen or sixteen inches behind the head, which was, without any doubt, that of a snake, and it was never, during the twenty minutes that it continued in sight of our glasses, once below the surface of the water; its color a dark brown with yellowish white about the throat. It had no fins, but something like a mane of a horse, or rather a bunch of seaweed, washed about its back. It was seen by the quartermaster, the boatswain's mate, and the man at the wheel, in addition to myself and officers above mentioned (Midshipman Sartoris, Lieutenant Edgar Drummond, William Barrett).

An extremely well-authenticated encounter with a sea serpent was reported in the *British Proceedings of the Zoological Society* in 1906 by fellows of the society, E. G. B. Meade-Waldo and Michael J. Nicoll. They were aboard the yacht *Valhalla*, owned by the Earl of Crawford, which was cruising off the coast of Brazil. The two naturalists were on the *Valhalla*'s poop at 10:15 A.M., December 7, 1905, when Nicoll pointed out what he thought was the fin of a large fish. Meade-Waldo saw what looked to be a "large fin or frill" sticking out of the water, crinkled at the edge and brown in color.

He focused his field glasses on it, and at the same instant a great head or neck rose out of the water in front of the fin but not touching it. The neck seemed to be about as thick as a small man's body and seven to eight feet of it was out of water. Under the water he could see a large-sized body. He later described the eye and the edge of the neck as "turtle-like."

In the *Proceedings*, Nicoll wrote approximately the same description as Nicole-Waldo, and said, "I feel sure, however, that it is not a reptile that we saw, but a mammal. It is, of course, impossible to be certain of this, but the general appearance of the creature, especially the soft, almost rubber-like fin, gave one this impression."

What is this mysterious monster of the seas whose existence many zoologists still refuse to credit? There is evidence that it is not a reptile but a mammal, but whichever it is, apparently it is not a serpent at all. Instead, it seems to have a rather bulky body with four large flippers which propel it through the water.

In 1849, Captain George Hope of Her Majesty's Ship *Fly*, was cruising in the Gulf of California in a perfectly calm sea. The water was transparent. and he could see a large animal swimming along the bottom. It had a longer neck than an alligator, and instead of legs it had four flippers which moved clumsily, like a turtle's. The front flippers were much larger than the hind flippers.

Using this as a basis, we can reconstruct the appearance of this strange creature. It is smooth-skinned, dark brown. Some varieties (or perhaps the male sex) have a soft rubbery fin or "frill" on their backs. It has a long neck and serpent-like head, and a long tail.

But Is It Reptile or Mammal?

Those zoologists who believe that it may exist say it is probably a mammal. The skin, and the fact that it is seen most often in cold waters where reptiles would be very sluggish, lead them to this conclusion.

In either case, there are very serious discrepancies—the most important of which is "Why are these creatures not seen more often? Why are they so rare that none has ever been taken by a whaler, for example?"

The logical answer is that this is a creature of the deep seas, that it lives most of the time in the great unknown depths of enormous pressures and lightless days. But if that is true, from whence does it derive its oxygen?

Could it possibly be a kind of fish, with gills capable of absorbing oxygen from sea water?

That would really upset zoology, because no creature with flippers has ever been known that also had gills. Could it, then, be an amphibian of some kind? The answer to that is that no amphibian so far known lives in salt water, or ever did, even in prehistoric times.

Another explanation might be that this is a creature of Arctic and Antarctic waters, where ships seldom penetrate, and only rarely does it leave its frozen fastness to venture out, or be carried by currents to warmer areas.

Until the fortunate day when one of these creatures is captured, all these suppositions must remain pure speculation. But the evidence is very clear, beyond contradiction of all but a few incurable skeptics, that "the great sea serpent" does exist. That it isn't really a serpent doesn't change the fact that capture of a live specimen would be the greatest zoological triumph of the century.

Sea Serpents and Whachamacallits

Ivan T. Sanderson

January 1964

A recent sighting of a forty-foot long, eel-like creature off the New Jersey coast raises a question—Is there more than one kind of sea monster?

A tendency has grown up over the past century to relate all oddities and enigmas to the department of midsummer madness, regardless of their seasonableness or their nature, including all unidentified animals, of any size, seen or alleged to have been seen in the sea.

While a healthy skepticism is necessary, some degree of objectivity is still desirable in the investigation of and reporting on anything, most particularly anything that appears to be odd or previously unknown. The day when humanity confidently believed it knew the limits of everything in the natural world has now passed.

A new look at our earth has led to a reappraisal of a number of old Silly Season saws—among them reports of large, unknown, unidentified kinds of animals, some of which our ancestors initially called the Great Sea Serpent. In due course, however, as reports came tumbling in, the expression "sea serpents" became accepted. Then, as more and more captains of ships and other "reliable" persons reported flippers, manes, and other appurtenances not possibly attributable to serpents or snakes, the "creatures"—hallucinatory or real—became known simply as Sea Monsters. And there the matter rested until the week of August 19, 1963.

On that day something was sighted off the New Jersey coast. As reported by John C. Devlin of the *New York Times* on August 20, this creature appeared to be glassy and almost wholly transparent, about forty feet long, and traveling at a good clip by "an undulatory" motion.

The initial sighting was made by none other than Dr. Lionel A. Walford, Director of the Fish and Wildlife Research Center of the United States Department of the Interior, Sandy Hook, New Jersey Among many other distinctions, Dr. Walford is a member of the Shark Research Panel. One does not, or at least should not, scoff at such a report given by such a person. What is more, one should read carefully just what he said, and for more than one good reason.

First, and perhaps most fascinating, was his insistence that he not be quoted as saying that he had seen a "sea serpent." He said, as reported by John Devlin, "Please be careful not to call it a sea serpent." This should raise a worldwide cheer from scientists and others who labor to get at the truth about the age-old reports of unknown animals in the sea.

Nevertheless, some pretty appalling things got into print, although the initial story is a model of good reporting:

"It was at least forty feet long and about five inches thick and perhaps seven to eight inches deep—looking something like an enormously long, flattened eel. It is (was) an invertebrate. It looked like so much jelly. I could see no bones, and no eyes, nose, or mouth. But, there it was, undulating along looking as if it were almost made of fluid glass" (*New York Times*, August 20, 1963).

One could not wish for more, considering the fact that this was what has come to be called a "sighting." The report continued:

"A number of us saw it. I didn't see it at first because I was busy with our project, but when the thing was pointed out to me—there it was. It was somewhat difficult to see because it was transparent. But I finally made a tentative identification of it as what is known as a *Venus Girdle*, a jelly-like creature . . . . However, upon examining my scientific references, I soon and surprisingly determined that the *Venus Girdle* does not grow longer than a few feet. And no amount of research I could do provided me with a proper identification of this strange creature."

What is a professional zoologist to do when confronted with such an extraordinary sight? His only appeal is to current knowledge in textbooks.

A word should be said on Dr. Walford's significant statement that "It is an invertebrate." The true significance of this escaped all but zoologists and high school biology students.

But first consider Reporter Devlin's sad lapse. He states blandly, "Sea Serpents, once the favorite subject of tall stories by mariners—or in more recent years the Loch Ness monster apparently conjured up by a press agent—have divided scientific opinion. They would be vertebrates."

I have on file few printed statements that include more nonsense in so short a space. It seems inconceivable that a top-notch reporter could have lived till this day without hearing of the discoveries made at Loch Ness by scientific groups from leading universities, by the British Navy, and by innumerable other groups or, alternatively, of similar creatures reported in the glacial lakes of Sweden, Canada, and other countries.

We need not discuss this further, apart from asking where and who the "press agent" was who set up a Loch Ness monster for Saint Columba in the year A.D. 565, and we would like to know who said, and on what grounds, "sea serpents" and the "Loch Ness monster" were, are, or must be vertebrates.

This brings me back to the most significant aspect of the current case—the statement: "It was an invertebrate."

There has been a grave and growing suspicion among interested scientists, naturalists, reporters, and other amateur viewers who say they have seen the Loch Ness and other lake, river, and sea "monsters" that at least some of them appear not to be vertebrated (without backbones). Some of the sketches made by observers and even some of the photos seem to bear this out. Moreover, it is just the lack of eyes, nose, and/or mouth, as reported by Dr. Walford, that strengthens the suggestion that they are invertebrates.

It is bad enough to be asked to assume there are large, unidentified animals in the oceans, seas, lakes, and rivers of the world. It is even worse to be asked to accept the fact that there are several different kinds of them. But to ask even a zoologist to accept the notion that some of them could be invertebrates seems to be pushing the point too far. Yet, if we are going to accept any possibility, and try to be logical, we have to consider this seemingly wild idea.

Take the case of a Mr. and Mrs. Price who, in 1933—just after the first road around Loch Ness had been opened and when, as a result, its "monster" first burst upon the modern world—said they had almost run into an "unknown" at night in their small car. They submitted a sketch of what they saw, or thought they saw, that showed a blob-sbaped mass with a long wormlike neck, no noticeable eyes but two short horns or tentacles and something sticking up behind that could have been the tip of a blunt tail, the end of a limb, or something else.

Take, also, the great mass of something at first said to be twenty feet long and almost as broad that lay about on a beach on the western shores of the island of Tasmania two years ago. It, too, was almost formless and displayed no sign of bones, limbs, or sense organs. Consider, again, a great thing seen hightailing it across the surface of the Gulf of Arabia without visible means of propulsion.

Then come down to earth and have a look at some of the giant invertebrates that we do know. We think of animals without backbones as all being small. However, the biggest known jellyfish (*Cyanea arctica*) can be as big as a horse and weigh almost a ton; and the largest of all non-vertebrated animals is the Giant Squid (*Architeuthis*) which weighs several tons and, when stretched out, may measure over forty feet. Animals buoyed up by water do not need solid girders to support them internally, and there seems to be almost no limit to their size in water. The mighty Blue Whale (a vertebrate) has been measured at over 113 feet, which represents an estimated (by the modern formula of one and a half tons per foot of length) almost 170 tons. There is actually no reason animals without backbones could not grow to the same size.

The question of what order of boneless animals these large unknowns might be is not an easy one to answer. I must ask you to trust me when I state that of the twenty-six currently recognized major groups (called Phyla) of animals, only four could, as far as we presently know, fit the specifications of these lake and sea "monsters." So far, we know of really giant examples of only one of these groups. These are the Giant Squids or Krakens among the mollusks or shellfish. But, the very fact that an octopus-like shellfish can grow to this size shows plainly what other groups may or could achieve.

There are those who have insisted that what they saw looked more like a giant slug than anything else. Dr. Walford states that his creature looked more like a "jellyfish." The thing on the beach in Tasmania looked like nothing known but could well have been a monster form of any of half a dozen groups.

Apart from the shellfish, and the group of so-called "jelly-fishes" known as the Coelenterata, which includes the vast *Cyanea arctica*, there are two obscure groups known as the Acorn Worms and the Echiuroids. The first are not in any way "worms" for they have a rodlike internal support that might be the prototype of a vertebral column. The second absolutely defeat me. They are bag-shaped things with long serpentine necks or tentacles in front, called delightfully "extroverts" (believe it or not), with which the animal reaches out ahead and then drags its cumbersome body forward. This device often has two soft horn-like structures or tentacles at its front end. There is then an organ for eliminating wastes from the body, but this, instead of being at the back end, is set off to the side. In fact, blow this animal up several thousandfold—for the biggest known is just over eighteen inches long—and you have almost exactly what Mr. and Mrs. Price swear they saw crossing the road alongside Loch Ness!

Some of the so-called Acorn Worms look much the same, with bulbous bodies and long "necks." What is more, some of them can move about by jet propulsion like the Giant Squids. They fill their body cavities with water and then squirt it out of their anuses with great force and so dart forward. If giant ones have developed they might, like the squids, be able to maintain a continuous forward drive such as has been reported time and time again of the great Whachamacallits, and which is common to squids. But what of the reported "undulatory motion"?

Here only the Ctenophores—jellylike and often transparent, please note—seem to fit the bill. Also, they are open water and often surface water creatures. If there are very, very large ones they could look just like what Dr. Walford and his companions saw.

However. the essential fact the non-professional monster hunter should endeavor to grasp is that "The world is full of a number of things." Nothing is simple in nature. There is no such thing as "The Whale." There are well over 100 different kinds of whales, ranging in size from over 100 feet to less than four feet when full-grown. There are dozens of known species of "cats," why should there be only one kind of "Sea Monster" or Whachmacallit? Couldn't there be dozens, or scores, or hundreds? After all, we have made only a very small beginning in our exploration of the bottoms of the oceans that cover almost three-quarters of the surface of our planet, and these oceans average over two miles in depth! Compound the volume of this mass of watery unknown before you deny what it can or cannot contain.

The Silly Season may, in fact, have given us the break we have been waiting for in this field of inquiry—thanks to the bold Dr. Walford who was not afraid to state for the record what he saw. This is most refreshing in this sad age of unwarranted scepticism and marvelous discovery. The next thing you know, he will have a Whatchamacallit on his lab table, just as Dr. Smith had a Coelacanth "fish" on his. Then we will have to begin all over again.

Morgawr, The Cornish Sea Serpent

Robert J. M Rickard
October 1977

"I could see a worm-like shape about forty feet long, its neck eight feet out of the water. I had never seen anything like it."

Cornwall, England's southwesternmost county, always has been shrouded in mystery and legend. It is said to be haunted by giants, ghosts, devils, witches, demon hounds, and piskies (the Cornish fairies) and its coasts hide sunken cities, mermaids, and sea monsters. These beliefs in magic and supernatural events have survived the coming of the automobile and the railways. Today Cornwall is still mystically remote, a land in which anything might happen and sometimes does.

Since the autumn of 1975 there have been intermittent reports of a large unknown creature in the waters of Falmouth Bay. The ancient Cornish distrust of outsiders kept many of these reports from surfacing and they would have passed into oblivion if it had not been for the efforts of one man, my friend Tony "Doc" Shiels, who pursued "Morgawr" (an old Cornish word meaning "sea giant") and collected accounts of its appearance until one day he finally came face to face with it himself.

The first sighting took place one September evening when two residents of Falmouth saw a large lumpy creature in the sea below Pendennis Point. Its ugly head had stumpy "horns" and its long neck was ridged with bristles. The couple watched the beast dive and resurface with a large conger eel in its mouth. The incident occurred two months before Dr. Robert Rines released his celebrated Loch Ness photographs which showed a "monster" with remarkably similar features.

Shortly after that several fishermen saw the monster out at sea and later blamed it for their recent bad catches, lousy weather, and general ill luck. They refused to go to sea again until it had been killed, captured or driven away. Needless to say, the press had fun at their expense.

Then in January 1976 a large carcass washed ashore on Durgan Beach sparking popular speculation that the monster had expired. But the body most certainly belonged to one of the many species of porpoise or small whale that swim in British coastal waters.

But soon events took an even more spectacular turn, if one credits an account published in the *Falmouth Packet* on March 5, 1976. A Falmouth woman who signed her name

"Mary F" wrote the newspaper saying that one day in February she had been walking on Trefusis Point and had seen a large unknown animal in the water below. Her sighting was different from the others in that she took two pictures of the creature. She described a black or dark brown body, fifteen to eighteen feet at the waterline, with a small snake-like head weaving about on the end of a long neck. Mary said the beast moved in a weird fashion and the eerie way the humps rippled frightened her so much that she ran from the scene.

Critics have disputed Mary F's claim that the photographs depict a living creature, pointing out that the figure is riding too high on the water in apparent defiance of the laws of gravity. Moreover, the background and foreground are so washed out that it is impossible to compare the "monster's" size to its immediate environment. Believers retort that the creature may have been standing in shallow water with sunlight reflecting off the waves.

In any case publication of the story prompted several other people to write the paper describing strikingly similar sightings. Two individuals on separate occasions said they first had thought they were looking at a "dead whale" when suddenly it slowly raised the tapering neck Mary F had desribed and its double-humped body sank below the choppy surface of Falmouth Bay. Another witness, Amelia Johnson, saw "a sort of prehistoric dinosaur" surface off Rosemullion Head. By the time she had pointed it out to her sister, it was gone and Johnson returned to London convinced she had imagined it. After her sister mailed her a clipping of Mary F's photographs, Amelia Johnson sent in her own account.

By mid-March Morgawr had become something of a local celebrity. Outside the county, however, she received only scant attention and the few references in the national press snickered that Cornwall might be trying to divert some of the silly-season traffic from Lochs Ness and Morar, where more famous monsters reputedly dwell. Doc Shiels, whose own background in Fortean research led him to suspect there was something more to Morgawr than that, began collecting information and even started his own monster watches along the coast.

On April Fool's Day one of the local papers engineered a stunt that effectively put an end to serious reporting of the sightings. It had a boat tug a huge inflated replica of a monster into Falmouth harbor. Everyone had a good laugh and the skeptics, of whom there were a great many, were relieved to have an excuse to dismiss any further reports out of hand. The scoffers were further aided by the antics of one Professor (of metaphysics) Michael McCormick, an American showman who told a press conference that he and Doc were going to summon the beast telepathically and capture it for display in his "Matchbox Circus." He brought along a few exhibits, most notably a "petrified basilisk" and the skeleton of an "imp," but departed at the end of the month without Morgawr. Doc, who as a stage magician and accomplished showman is not at all averse to personal publicity himself, went along with McCormick's nonsense because he found that the media attention encouraged people to come to him with stories they would not tell reporters:

Some of the stories were fantastic, indeed. For instance, two young sisters from Lancashire, June and Vicky Melling, told him they had seen a winged semihuman creature, the size of a man, at Mawnan Old Church, near the site of several reported appearances of Morgawr. Later several more witnesses to this bizarre "Owlman" came forward although the earlier stories had not been published in the press. (Nor for that matter were the later ones.)

A group of young witches informed Doc they too planned to summon the beast. They were going to do it by swimming naked in the Helford River on the pagan feast of

May Eve. As proof of their abilities they showed Doc photographs of "little people" they claimed to have summoned during one of their recent rites. On May Eve a huge crowd gathered on Grebe Beach, attracted more by the prospect of the beautiful young witches' nude dip than by the prospect of seeing Morgawr. Alas, neither event took place.

While at one of his observation posts Doc was approached by a schoolboy who insisted on remaining anonymous. He said he had a picture of Morgawr, "slimy black and about twenty-five feet long," moving up the Helford River. Unfortunately the photograph is badly out of focus.

On the morning of May 4 two young London bankers, Tony Rogers and John Chambers, were fishing from rocks on Parsons Beach when, as Rogers later recalled, "Suddenly something rose out of the water about 150 or 200 yards away. It was greeny-gray and appeared to have humps. Then another smaller one appeared. They were visible for about ten seconds and looked right at us." Chambers said that he did not see the smaller one himself and that neither of them ever had heard of Morgawr.

Perhaps fearing she had revealed too much, Morgawr lay low for exactly two months. When she reappeared on July 4 the witness was none other than Doc Shiels himself.

Doc had taken his family for an early morning swim at Grebe Beach. As usual he had brought his binoculars along, not really expecting to see the monster but nonetheless routinely checking out anything suspicious in the Helford estuary just in case. When suddenly he saw the familiar double-humped, long-necked form of Morgawr about 500 yards away he was unable to credit his senses. At first he did not even dare call to his wife and two children. Finally after he had observed it for a while, he got their attention and they all watched the creature appear and disappear several times. Doc's wife Christine wrote an account for the *Packet* (July 9, 1976) because Doc suspected no one would believe the story from him.

In fact he wasn't even sure he would believe a story from him. After all, the sighting had occurred in the middle of the longest, hottest, driest English summer in 200 years and he wondered if he and his family had not suffered some kind of heat-induced hallucination out of their desire to see the beast for themselves. Secretly Doc hoped for another chance to meet the elusive Morgawr.

The same edition of the *Packet* which published Christine Shiels' letter also reported that a hotel worker, Roy Peters, had seen something even stranger while skin-diving off Grebe Beach a few days earlier. Peters claimed he had startled three "serpent-like things," each about five feet long, as they swam at a leisurely pace just beneath the surface of the water.

"They had skin like seals," he said, "but because of their ugly heads and necks (they) definitely were not seals." Peters chased them but lost them in nearby weed beds.

Two dramatic sightings occurred farther out to sea.

In the First John Cook and George Vinnicombe were fishing twenty-five miles south of Lizard Point, an interesting name that hints of similar phenomena in antiquity. The sea was flat and calm and the two men could see for several miles. But when Morgawr suddenly appeared she was so close that, as Vinnicombe put it, "if we had not reversed engines we would have been right on top of it.

"It looked like an enormous tire about four feet up in the water with a back like corrugated iron. We must have woken it up because a great head, like an enormous seal, came out of the water. I've been fishing for forty years and have seen nothing like it. It just turned its long neck and looked at us and very slowly submerged." He estimated its visible length at tewnty-two feet and its weight at several tons.

The other incident occurred to Patrick Dolan, a well-known art historian and single-handed sailing enthusiast from Cardiff, Wales. He had left Falmouth on July 9 and by July 11 was some thirty miles north-northwest of the Scilly Isles, en route to Kinsdale, Ireland. Just before sunset he saw a peculiar disturbance in the water. Later he wrote to the *Packet* (September 24, 1976), "I could see quite distinctly a kind of worm-like shape in the water and the neck was about eight feet out of the water. It was about forty feet long and propelled itself with an undulating movement. It overtook me at about ten to twelve knots. I have never seen anything like this. I just have had it in my vision for about twenty minutes."

Morgawr surfaced in Carrick Roads on August 27 not just once but three times in ten minutes. Twelve days later she was seen looking like an "upturned boat," drifting toward Gyllyngness Beach. As it got nearer the witness saw a creature "like a giant eel" with a hump formation on its back.

One of the stranger sightings took place on September 12. A brother and sister, Alan and Sally White, were holidaying near Grebe Beach. That morning they were walking along the beach when something large and odd slid into the sea ahead of them. In their initial confusion they thought it was a dog but when they were able to sort out their impressions they realized the "dog" was about fifteen to twenty feet long.

For his part Doc was beginning to feel discouraged. While all these sightings were going on elsewhere, Morgawr seemed to be evading his vigils at Grebe Beach. Doc had just about concluded that he would never see the creature again. Then on the morning of November 17, as he wandered near Parsons Beach below Mawnan talking with *Cornish Life* editor David

Clarke about a matter of mutual interest having nothing to do with the fabled Morgawr, they met again.

Shiels and Clarke's conversation was interrupted by a disturbance in the Helford River about 100 yards away. As they looked Morgawr appeared. They could see clearly the smallish head with stumpy horns and a large mouth opening and closing and they further noted the double-humped back other witnesses had mentioned. As Morgawr steamed up the estuary the two recovered their wits and aimed their cameras. Clarke had a telephoto lens and could see Morgawr in detail but his camera jammed and delivered useless double and triple exposures. Doc managed to get three shots before Morgawr sank.

These three photographs had to be taken in haste and were not the definitive proof Doc had hoped for. However, they do indicate a movement, a water displacement by a large submerged body, and a splendid wake, and are convincing indeed.

While slightly disappointed, Doc was satisfied to know he finally had seen it again, more clearly and in the company of a man whose judgment he respected. "I've done what I said I'd do," he wrote to me. "I've captured the beastie—on film! All good sympathetic magicians should know what that means. This image should give me a certain amount of power according to standard magical practice. If my theatrical dragon-invoking antics really caused the monster to appear it should be possible to repeat the experiment."

But Doc now had less motive to perform the "experiment" again. Convinced of the reality of Morgawr, he doubts whether any number of materializations before their very lenses would ever persuade the press and the scientific establishment that one or more large, unknown aquatic animals live within a day's travel from the British Museum in London.

No Interest Elsewhere

The only real interest outside Falmouth has been the quiet reaction of a few of Britain's top monster hunters. Peter Costello, author of *In Search of Lake Monsters*, wrote the Packet to point out that Mary F's photographs are the first record of a living sea monster. Tim Dinsdale, author and experienced expedition leader, visited Falmouth for a while and was impressed with Doc's pictures, which he thinks are authentic. F. W. Holiday, author of the controversial *The Dragon and the Disc*, finds much in Morgawr to support his radical view that such monsters may not be normal physical creatures but merely one of a whole spectrum of related paranormal phenomena which also include "Owlmen," UFOs, and other assorted bizarre manifestations.

Allowing for the variations in reported size and coloring—we may be dealing with more than one creature—the descriptions of Morgawr tally with one another and also with those associated with the Nessie-type monster which has been reported around the world. The resemblance even stretches to the peculiar land sightings, the disturbing manner of movement, and the equipment malfunctions at critical moments (frequently reported by investigators of UFOs and psychic phenomena). The best-informed guesses about the identity of Nessie—variously thought to be an enormous worm, a giant eel, a long-necked seal, or a surviving plesiosaur—also apply to Morgawr.

The major problems with these suggestions, all extrapolations from conventional zoology, is that none of them explains how such animals could have remained undetected, except for sporadic sightings, for centuries while still maintaining the numbers necessary to survive as a successful breeding group. Because the coast of Britain is heavily traveled, sightings should have been far more frequent.

Perhaps significantly the same has been said of other sporadically sighted animals such as Bigfoot, the yeti and Surrey's elusive "puma"—creatures that seem to live a phantom existence. They come and go like ghosts leaving no physical evidence of their activity or whereabouts between appearances.

Charles Fort liked to speculate that these animals engaged in teleportation—travel through time or space without physically traversing the intervening distance. Holiday's refinement of this notion is that these creatures may not be "real" animals but a kind of *genius loci*, traditionally believed to be a phantom associated with certain locations which materializes and dematerializes according to laws we have yet to discover. Obviously we need a great deal more evidence before we have any answers.

The late Fortean writer Harold T. Wilkins saw an awfully strange sight on July 5, 1949, as he and a friend walked one morning along the Cornish coast at East Looe. In a footnote in his 1958 book *Strange Mysteries of Time and Space* Wilkins wrote they had seen "two remarkable saurians, nineteen to twenty feet long, with bottle-green heads, one behind the other, their middle parts under the water of the tidal creek, apparently chasing a shoal of fish up the creek. What was amazing were their dorsal parts, ridged, serrated, and like the old Chinese pictures of dragons. Gulls swooped down towards the one in the rear which had a large piece of orange peel on his dorsal parts. These monsters . . . resembled the plesiosaurus of Mesozoic times."

Wilkins suffered the fate of most prophets: he was ignored. A national newspaper to which he sent the report refused to publish it. He was twenty-seven years ahead of his time.

A letter published in the *Packet* for March 12, 1976, reminded readers of an old pub in Falmouth, long since demolished, called "The Dolphin."

"Over the fireplace," the writer said, "hung a replica sea serpent which as the story goes was frequently seen in Falmouth Bay in the days of sail."

Oh, the stories those Cornish pubs must have heard—and oh, for a time machine!

My Escape from a Sea Monster

Edward Brian McCleary
May 1965

In back of us we could hear whatever it was, splashing and making that hissing sound.

March 24, 1962, was a warm, beautiful Saturday. I was having my morning coffee when the telephone rang. It was Eric Ruyle, a skin diving companion, calling to ask me to go with him and some friends on a skin diving expedition off the coast of Pensacola, Florida. I agreed to go after checking the morning paper for information on the day's tides and weather.

I had been living in Florida for about two years and I enjoyed the diving most of all. Now, for the first time, I had a chance to dive around a sunken ship. Eric had said we would dive at a sunken ship near Pensacola Bay. I had not seen the boat before but I pictured its open passages with fish swimming in and out, with moss-like growth hanging from its decks, and the whole ship covered by the blue-green Gulf of Mexico.

I collected my gear and walking out the front door smelled the fresh, clear air of spring mixed with the salt spray from the ocean. There was not a cloud in the sky. The white sand ran for miles down the beach, reflecting the morning sun like a mirror. As I stood there with the sun warming my back and heating the morning I knew this was a perfect day for skin diving.

A dilapidated Ford pulled into my driveway. It was Eric, Warren Sullay, Brad Rice, and Larry Bill. We drove off toward Pensacola and a sunken ship called the *Massachusetts*. The boys told me it was on a sandbar about two miles off the coast.

We had a seven-foot Air Force life raft tied to the top of the car. It had a drift anchor, pockets for provisions, and oars. We planned to use it to get us back and forth to the ship.

In a little over half an hour we arrived at Ft. Pickens State Park. The park is right across the bay from Pensacola and was a gun installation during the Civil War. The *Massachusetts* lay just off the coast. We climbed the three stories of the main embattlement, a long rectangular structure with a square brick tower on top of which is mounted a telescope. Through the telescope I scanned the horizon and saw an object sticking out of the water, just off the coast—the *Massachusetts*.

We changed into our suits, loaded all our equipment into the raft and carried it down to the beach. I waded into the water but came out quickly. It was very cold. We thrust the raft into the foam and cleared the small waves with ease. The water was calm.

On the way out to the ship we took turns paddling so no one would be tired for the diving. When I was relieved I sat back and lit a cigarette. A small wind was coming down from the north, cooling the air. Down in the water I could see the beams of sunlight piercing the surface to plunge below and become lost in the green depths. I guessed the visibility at about forty feet underwater. I thought I would stand the cold to get into that fascinating world. My daydream was interrupted by Larry. "Hey, we're not going any place. When we took off the ship was on our right, now it's on the left."

"So paddle the other way," Eric said. "You gotta make up for the drifts and tides."

"Somebody relieve me," Warren huffed, "this water's rough. My arm's killing me."

The water had, in fact, become topped with small whitecaps which lapped against the side of our raft. I shifted my attention from the water to the sky. The blue now was overshadowed by some gray clouds which hid the sun and gave the water a dull blue color. The seagulls were skimming across the top of the waves toward shore. The salty breeze seemed stronger by the minute.

"Looks like we won't do much diving today. Storm's coming up. Looks like it anyhow. We'd better get back to shore," Warren said.

We spun the raft around and started paddling back to shore, which by now was a thin green strip in the north, harder to see each passing minute. Because of the wind the waves were washing us into the bay channel, which extended out into the open sea.

In an attempt to keep from being dragged into the open water Eric, Warren, and I jumped into the icy water and began kicking behind the raft. Larry and Brad took the oars. But the tide was too strong for us. We climbed back into the raft, shivering and cramped from the numbing cold. The waves were so high by this time we had to hold onto the sides of the raft to stay upright.

As the sky grew darker the small craft in the area began to desert the open water for safety in port. Just entering the channel was a small Chris Craft. We thought it would be our last chance to get to shore safely so we all stood up and yelled "Mayday." It was difficult to yell, wave, and keep our balance at the same time. On the deck of the boat was an elderly woman. At first she didn't notice us. Then she glanced in our direction and waved.

"We're saved! She's seen us. Hey, over here. Mayday! Mayday!" we yelled. The boat did not veer from its course.

Brad grabbed the shark gun, tied his red shirt around the tip, unhooked the line, and fired it directly at the boat. The kick from the gun knocked him over and the raft almost overturned. The spear hurled through the damp air and landed about fifty feet short of the boat. It was impossible for anybody to miss the distress signal. But the boat creased into the channel, headed back into port.

"We're lost. Damn those fools. We're lost. We'll drown," Larry wailed.

"Look, we're not lost yet. There's a buoy over there." I pointed out into the channel, a mile distant."We'll tie onto it with the drag anchor as we go by. We'll be okay. No reason to get shook up."

We tried to paddle to the buoy. The waves were beginning to swamp the raft. Only the inflatable sides kept us afloat. The five of us were sitting, numb from the cold, in a pool of icy brine. At last we came close to the buoy. We were in for a shock. A massive edifice of steel loomed above us like an angry giant. Its worn, chipped, red paint contrasted with the black sky. It was covered with seaweed from top to bottom.

As the waves lifted it from its mooring a great riptide was formed at the bottom. The water foamed, gurgled, and was sucked underneath the metal monster. All twenty feet of it looked down on us. I stood up and hurled the anchor at the buoy like a lasso. But before the line had a chance to reach the buoy the raft was caught in the undertow and dragged right for the bottom of the buoy. It was like going down hill in a roller coaster.

"Jump!" I yelled, and just in time. As the last man hit the water the whole thing came down full force on the raft, dragging it under. I surfaced, spitting water and gasping for breath.

"Over here. The raft came up over here," Warren yelled. Eric and I were the first to reach it. We got everything out and threw it overboard. We turned the raft over and managed to get most of the water out. The rest climbed back in; we clung to the sides. The rain began to lash down like icy needles. The sky was black as night. Just as we left the channel we were dragged past the ship where we had intended to dive.

The wheelhouse which stuck out of the water was being battered by the waves. The winds roared through the open windows of the bridge, making a noise like the wail of sirens. Back and forth the cabin lunged, rocked by the mighty sea.

Sometime later, I don't know how long, the sheets of rain became a fine mist. The sea subsided, tapering off finally to the calmness of a mountain lake. Out of nowhere a thick fog rolled across the water blanketing us in the stuffy, moist atmosphere of an undiscovered tomb. Not a wave rippled, not a fish broke water, not a seagull called. Silence hung on the fog.

For the first time in my life I was really scared. While I was sitting there I felt a big, icy hand grab me around the chest and squeeze. My stomach froze; my heart skipped and cold chills ran down my legs. We were exhausted from fighting the storm and the present atmosphere made matters worse.

Brad began to whimper, "We're dead. We died in that storm. Oh God, why did it happen to me?"

"No, no, we're fine; nothing to worry about; calm down. We'll be back to land in a few hours," Eric tried to calm Brad.

After quieting Brad we tried to think what we could do. We decided we were helpless until the fog cleared and we could see where we were. Until then we could only wait. The fog showed no signs of lifting. Visibility was limited to twenty-five feet. There wasn't a whisper of wind.

I tried some small talk to break the tension. "Eric, see if the cigarettes got wet, will you?"

"No. There are two packs, nice and dry. The lighter works too. We're in luck."

We passed the cigarettes around and the tension seemed to subside. For some reason though, we all spoke softly.

"We better get back soon. I've got a date tonight," Brad said, grinning widely.

We all chuckled and felt a lot easier. But the conversation died down again and everyone was lost in his own thoughts.

The water was unusually warm beneath us, warm even for summer and this was March.

Larry bolted upright, saying, "Shhhh, I hear a boat or something."

We all listened for the noise he had heard. The misty air became filled with the odor of dead fish. My stomach heaved and I gasped for breath. just then, about forty feet away, we heard a tremendous splash. The waves reached the raft and broke over the side.

"What in the hell was that?" Larry asked.

"Whatever it was, it wasn't any boat. That's for sure," Eric said.

Again we heard the splash and now, through the fog we could make out what looked like a telephone pole. It was about ten feet high, with a bulb on the top. It stood erect for a moment and then bent in the middle and dove under. The sickening odor filled the air.

"I've never seen anything like that in my life. What do you think it was?" I whispered.

"Maybe it was an oarfish. I've heard that they look like snakes," Warren answered.

"Oarfish don't stand straight up," Brad said.

"Maybe it's a sea monster," I suggested.

Everyone looked at me in silence. We all had been thinking the same thing. I was just the first to say it.

The silence was broken once again by something out in the fog. I can only describe it as a high-pitched whine. We panicked. All five of us put on our fins and dove into the water. Patches of brown, crusty slime lay all over the surface. I began to swim and kick spasmodically. I felt a small curent under the surface and I hoped it would carry me in the direction of the shore.

"Keep together. Stay behind me and try for the ship," I yelled. Eric and I were swimming together. The rest were together behind us. We made pretty good time at first. Our fear was indescribable.

In back of us we could hear whatever it was, splashing and making that hissing sound. The fog was clearing some and the water was becoming a bit rougher. Darkness was closing in. The rain began once more and the water was losing its warmth. I began to take long, slow mechanical strokes to keep me afloat, for I was becoming cramped. Eric was still nearby. Every so often we would call back to make sure the group was all right.

I don't know how long it was before we heard a scream. It lasted maybe half a minute. Then I heard Warren call, "Hey! Help me! It's got Brad! It got Brad! I've got to get outta here . . . ." His voice was cut off abruptly by a short cry.

"Brad, Warren. Hey! Where is everybody?" I yelled back at the top of my lungs. Larry now swam with Eric and me. Warren and Brad were nowhere in sight.

The only sounds now were those of the sea and the lightning. I had an eerie feeling—swimming in a storm, not knowing how many feet of ocean were beneath me, what was down there waiting for me. I wanted to sink into the green silence. I felt all alone, peaceful and quiet. It would have been so easy just to surrender to the sea, but something inside me kept going. The pain in my legs was like fire but I kept up the mechanical strokes. I knew I had to keep going.

When at last I realized where I was again Larry was gone.

"Eric, what happened to Larry? He was here a minute ago."

"I don't know. He was just here."

Both of us dove for him, tried to see if we couldn't get him to the surface but there was no trace of him. After a while we had to give up. Then Eric grimaced and sank. I swam over and wrapped his arm around my neck. "Cramps," he said.

We swam like this for what must have been a couple of hours. I hoped we were going in the right direction. It was pitch dark. The waves were breaking on my head. My lungs were filled with salt water. I was ready to give up. Eric was becoming heavier by the minute and I had no hope. Just as I was going under the lightning flashed and I saw the silhouette of the *Massachusetts*. I began to take stronger strokes. We were saved.

"Come on, Eric," I said, "we'll be okay, boy. The ship's just over the next wave. I've got to keep up. Come on, baby, let's go."

I was close to the ship when a giant wave pulled me under and yanked Eric's arm from around my neck. I came up and couldn't see him anywhere. Then lightning flashed and I saw him ahead of me. He was afloat and swimming for the ship.

Right next to Eric that telephone pole-like figure broke water. I could see the long neck and two small eyes. The mouth opened and it bent over. It dove on top of Eric, dragging him under. I screamed and began to swim past the ship. My insides were shaking uncontrollably.

I do not know what happened after that. The *Massachusetts* is two miles from shore but I do not remember swimming this distance after Eric was killed. I thought I went down, down. I thought I rested on the soft sandy bottom. Voices talked to me. I felt warm and secure. I was at peace. I knew I was dead.

I couldn't believe it when I felt sand under my feet and the silence of my peaceful "death" was shattered by pounding surf. I was flung forward on my face and got a mouthful of sand. I tried to walk but kept falling to my knees. Then I remembered I had my fins on. I threw them back into the water and headed up the beach. I tried to find help. I could see the lights of Pensacola in the distance but I didn't know where I was. The cold night wind was making me shiver so I looked for a warm place. I finally came to a tower of some sort. I climbed all the way up the ladder and passed out on the floor of the little cabin. I must have slept about two hours but it seemed like two years. All night long I kept hearing voices.

I was awakened by the Sunday morning sun hitting my face through a window of the tower. I ached all over from the long swim. I got up and looked out the window, across the white beach, across the calm Gulf. The events of the previous day seemed like a bad dream. I headed for the ladder. My legs wouldn't support me and I fell down the ladder to land face down in the sand below. I was crawling across the sand when a group of boys came up to me.

"Say, Mister, you must be one of the divers lost yesterday."

"Yeah. I've got to get help. How did you know about the accident?"

"The coast guard found the raft this morning and began a search."

"I've got to get help . . . please."

The next thing I remember was waking up in the Pensacola Naval Base hospital. Breakfast was in front of me but I couldn't eat because my throat was sore from the salt water.

The director of the Search and Rescue units came in to see me that morning. Director E. E. McGovern was a mild-mannered, friendly Southerner. I remember him well because of his kind face. I told him exactly what happened, what I had witnessed.

"Did they find any of the others?" I asked him.

"No," he replied. "We've had planes out all mornin' and we've been combin' the beaches but we haven't found nothin' yet."

"Do you believe me, about what happened and all?" I asked.

"You know, son," he drawled, "the sea has a lot of secrets. There are a lot of things we don't know about. People don't believe these things because they're afraid to. Yes, I believe you. But there's not much else I can do."

He asked me some more questions and then he left.

Some reporters interviewed me later that day. After they had gone I wondered if I really believed what had happened. I thought it must have happened because the boys were dead. And I knew that thing that got them was real.

It is true. The sea has some terrible secrets, and now I know how she manages to keep them.

The Reports

Both the *Pensacola Journal* and *Playground News* of Ft. Walton carried stories of this tragedy. These stories do not match Brian McCleary's account of what the doctors at the Naval hospital had to say. One report says Brian "drifted and swam more than two miles" but Coast Guard and Navy rescue units estimated he swam five miles. Doctors at the Naval Base said he was in the water over twelve hours.

The interviewing reporters told Brian their stories would not mention the sea serpent as it was "better left unmentioned for all concerned."

The bodies of Eric Ruyle, Warren Sullay, and Larry Stuart Bill, were never recovered. One body washed ashore a week after the accident and Brian says, "To the best of my knowledge, I identified the body as that of Brad Rice."

The raft was found ten miles from where Brian came out of the water. He was picked up near Fort McRae about 7:45 a.m. Sunday, March 5, 1962, by a helicopter from the Naval Air Station. He had spent the early morning hours in an old gun emplacement.

The clipping further states Brian was suffering from shock and exposure but was released to his parents after brief treatment in the Naval hospital.

Brian writes us that after the accident he had a nervous breakdown but recovered and was able to resume his life in about three months.

Gigantic Ocean Creatures

The Search for Monster Sharks

Dr. Karl P. N. Shuker

March 1991

Is something more subtle, more dangerous, and many times larger than any shark we know lurking beneath the sea?

In 1976, near the Hawaiian island of Oahu, a mighty forteen-foot-long shark was accidentally hauled up from the sea. It proved to be so radically different from all others that it required the creation of an new scientific family of sharks. Its species was christened megamouth (*Megachama pelagios*) on account of its gigantic, cavernous maw and huge, rubbery lips.

Nothing like it had ever been seen before. Its discovery provided the most potent portent since the first living coelacanth was found in 1938 that the oceans still have a great variety of major ichthyological secrets awaiting disclosure. Among these may be a number of other sharks, some of very strange form and behavior judging from the tantalizing clues that have been documented over the years.

In August 1880, a still-unidentified creature that may have bearing upon the subject of mystery sharks was captured at New Harbor, Maine, by Captain S. W. Hanna. According to a *Sea-Side Press* report published at that time, "S. W. Hanna, of Pemaquid, caught what might be called a young sea serpent in his nets the other day. It was about twenty-five feet long and ten inches in diameter in the largest part, and was shaped like an eel. The head was flat, and the upper part projected out over the mouth, which was small and contained sharp teeth. It was dead when found."

This report attracted great interest, and U.S. Fish Commission ichthyologist Spencer Baird succeeded in obtaining more details from Captain Hanna regarding his curious catch (published in the Commission's *Bulletin for 1883*). He learned that its skin was very fine, like that of a dogfish or shark, that there was a pair of small fins laced a little way behind its head, and a single, triangular fin just above them, on its back. The only other fin present was a low tall fin, similar in shape to an eel's. Judging from a simple sketch prepared by Hanna, his fish seemed to have only three pairs of gills, uncovered like those of sharks (almost all modern-day sharks possess five pair, and a few have six or even seven). Its mouth was positioned at the very tip of its head instead of underneath, as with all other sharks known at that time. In a letter dated September 24, 1880, Baird regarded this fish as a representative of a totally new species, but as Hanna had not preserved it, its identity is as mysterious today as it was then.

At the time of its capture by Hanna, its snake-like (anguinine) shape, as well as its terminally sited mouth, lent support to the view that it was a peculiar type of eel rather than any shark. The mere concept of a shark fashioned on the above design seemed much too bizarre for serious contemplation until 1884.

Another Mystery Shark

From 1879 to 1881, Austrian naturalist Ludwig Doderlein brought to Vienna a collection of Japanese fishes that included two specimens of a very curious eel-like shark complete with a terminally positioned mouth, thus belonging to a species hitherto unrecorded by science. Investigations uncovered that this mysterious creature was familiar to Japanese long-line fishermen who refer to it as *tokagizame* ("lizard-head shark") and *ribuka* ("silk shark," possibly describing its soft scales and fins), and capture it at depths of 600 to 1,800 feet. Additional Japanese specimens were obtained during the next few years, followed by others from further afield.

In 1884, Samuel Garman formally described their species, and named it *Chlamydosclachus anguineus* ("snake-like shark with frills"). Referred to in popular parlance as the frilled shark, it has two conspicuous features. First, its body—measuring up to six and one-half feet in total length—is extremely slender, genuinely affording it an unexpectedly snake-like appearance. Second, six gills on each side of its throat have frilly edges. This is a unique feature among modern-day sharks but was exhibited by various primitive sharks dating back almost 400 rnilllon years to Duvonian times. A deep-water species that preys upon octopuses and squids, the frilled shark is distributed widely. It inhabits the Atlantic ocean and both sides of the Pacific ocean.

However, it is by no means a common species, and much of the lifestyle of the frilled shark remains unknown.

One of the most intriguing areas of speculation concerns its size. To date, the longest fully authenticated specimens do not exceed seven feet. However, if a frilled shark could attain a much greater length, its appearance would be remarkably similar to the description of a number of alleged sea serpents reported over the years.

Of great interest in relation to this is the putative sea serpent washed into Sydney Harbor during August 1907 and spotted by a Rose Bay fisherman who alerted Australian ichthyologist Dr. David G. Stead. When Stead arrived to examine it, all that the fisherman had been able to preserve was the creature's skull and approximately 150 of its backbone's vertebrae. Nevertheless, these were enough for Stead to be able to identify it confidently as a frilled shark. Based upon the number and size of the vertebrae, however, he was forced to seriously entertain the possibility that this specimen may have been at least ten feet long. Its discoverer attested that it had been at least twelve feet long.

If so, this virtually doubles the officially accepted maximum length for the frilled shark, and makes the likelihood of even longer individuals lurking beyond the visions of humans in the ocean's dark depths a lot less implausible than one might otherwise believe.

Since then, the possibility that Hanna's unidentified fish may in turn have belonged to some wholly unknown species of giant anguinine or serpentine shark, allied to the more diminutive frilled shark, has gained greater credence, culminating with the approval of sea serpent researcher Dr. Bernard Heuvelmans, expressed in his book *In the Wake of the Sea-Serpents*. Here the author reiterated that the existence of such forms would provide a satisfactory explanation for certain sea-serpent sightings.

The Strange Carpet Shark

The frilled shark is assuredly the quintessential strange shark among all of those currently known, but it is not the only one that may still have much larger and stranger relatives awaiting official recognition. In *The Lungfish and the Unicorn* (1948), Willy Ley mentioned that the Timor Sea, stretching between the island of Timor and Australia's northern coasts, is reputedly inhabited by a type of ferocious man-eating shark, apparently unlisted by science. According to native testimony it is larger than the true, man-eating shark (the great white shark) which also dwells in these waters and averages fourteen to fifteen feet long (rarely exceeding twenty feet).

In addition, Timor's mystery shark lacks the great white's most famous trademark, the high, triangular, dorsal fin. Instead, it has only a small, dorsal fin. Also, In contrast to the great white's preference for swimming near the surface of the sea, the mystery shark lies in wait for its victims on the sea bottom. Stemming from such behavior, the natives refer to this fish as the ground shark. What could it be?

As it happens, there is a very strange group of sharks whose members correspond very closely to the unidentified underwater denizen. Known as carpet sharks or wobbegongs (the aboriginal name given to their Australian representatives but also popularly applied to their Japanese and Chinese relatives) and measuring up to ten and a half feet in total length, they seem to epitomize everything that typical sharks are not. Typical sharks are sleek and swift; wobbegongs are flattened and sluggish. Indeed, they look more like rays or skates than sharks at first, but the location of their gill openings on the sides of their bodies (as in other sharks) readily differentiates them. Rays and skates bear their gills on their undersides.

Wobbegongs owe their "carpet" appellation in part to their coloration, a much-mottled, complicated combination of browns, reds, blacks, and grays, intermingled with spots and stripes. They resemble a richly patterned carpet. They also owe their name to their behavior.

In stark contrast to the active hunting techniques employed by most sharks, a wobbegong prefers to await a visit from its prey (generally consisting of fishes and crustaceans). Accordingly, it spends its days reposing langorously on the bottom of shallow seas, where its flat, dappled body blends perfectly with the complex shades of its seaweed-encrusted surroundings—it becomes an invisible carpet on the sea floor. It even bears unique frond-like flaps of skin around its head and mouth that break up its outline and greatly resemble tufts of seaweed, further enhancing its camouflage. When potential prey comes within reach, however, this seemingly inanimate "carpet" abruptly comes to life and seizes the hapless creature before it has even become aware of its plight.

There are a few verified cases on record involving attacks by wobbegongs on divers, but these unshark-like sharks are not generally looked upon as being dangerous to humans. However, what if there were much larger wobbegongs than those known to science? Perhaps there are. After all, the unclassified ground shark's lurking, sea-bottom lifestyle is characteristic of wobbegongs. Wobbegongs have not just one but two dorsal fins, but both are relatively small, inconspicuous structures near the rear end of the body, so they might not be readily seen by a human observer encountering a specimen beneath the water.

Could the mysterious ground shark of Timor truly be an unknown, giant species of wobbegong? The concept of enormous species of shark still eluding formal detection used to be dismissed as improbable, but then megamouth came along and shark skepticism hasn't been the same since.

A Freshwater Killer?

Another shark in search of an identity is the unnamed inhabitant of New Guinea's Lake Sentani. Natives living in the area of this large body of fresh water (about twenty miles inland from New Guinea's northern coast) fervently believe that it houses a number of sharks. To date, all such testimony has been rejected as erroneous by science.

Yet there is at least one report whose veracity is surely beyond all dispute. As reported by Dr. Heuvelmans (*Cryptozoology*, 1986), American anthropologist Dr. George Agogino was stationed at Lake Sentani during World War II, and needed to obtain some fresh fish to supply his army unit. He dropped a hand bomb into the lake in the hope of blasting some fishes out of the water. To his astonishment, a huge creature came to the surface, one that he could readily identify as a shark, measuring at least eleven feet long. He was even able to sketch it before it sank back beneath the waters.

Although not apparently unusual in appearance, its alleged occurrence in a freshwater lake is something of a novelty, as many people believe that sharks are exclusively marine. In fact, this is not totally true. There is one species that has actually become quite famous (or more accurately, notorious) for penetrating great distances inland via rivers and other stretches of fresh water. This singular shark is *Carcharhinus leucas*, the extremely aggressive bull shark. So far, it has been recorded in rivers and lakes as widely dispersed as Asia's Tigris, Euphrates, and Ganges Rivers, Africa's Zambezi, South America's Amazon River, Central America's Lake Nicaragua, North America's Atchafalaya River in Louisiana, the Mississippi, assorted bodies of fresh water in Australia and the Philippines, plus, of special note, the sizeable Lake Jamoer (Jamur) in New Guinea.

In view of the bull shark's known existence in Lake Jamoer, it would not be unreasonable to suppose that the Lake Sentani sharks are also of this species, or at least of a closely related one. So why should their very existence still be in dispute almost half a century after Dr. Agogino's sighting? Clearly this is a case in need of resolution by an intrepid ichthyologist.

The recent discovery of megamouth—we now have just four specimens from widely separated localities—has demonstrated very successfully that even a shark as large and novel as this one can indeed exist totally undetected by science. It also encourages speculation regarding the possible survival from prehistory into the present day of one of the most horrific sea creatures ever to have lived—a shark to end all sharks.

The Ultimate Monster Shark

It's long been known that from twenty-five million to one million years ago (Miocene to mid-Pleistocene times), the oceans contained a monstrous relative of the great white shark. Formally known as *Carcharodon megalodon*, and informally as megalodon ("big tooth"), its names refer to its huge teeth—triangular in shape, with serrated edges, and up to four inches long!

In 1909, their dramatic dimensions were used by scientists as the basis for early estimates of the shark's total length—eighty feet! The concept of a voraciously carnivorous shark only a little shorter than the gargantuan blue whale is horrifying. Happily, in more recent years further studies on fossilized megalodon remains have refined this estimate considerably, reducing it to a more sedate, yet still unnervingly formidable, forty-three feet in length.

Yet even this may not be the last word on the matter. Some extra-large megalodon teeth have been collected at the appropriately named Sharktooth Hill near Bakersfield, California. Based upon these ancient teeth—allegedly measuring almost six inches long—it is possible that some of these spectacular sharks actually attained lengths of up to a full fifty-five feet.

So far, megalodon has been treated as a wholly extinct species. There are tantalizing ripples running through zoological literature, however, which intimate that the oceans may not have outlived this colossal creature after all!

In 1875, the British oceanographic survey vessel *Challenger* dredged up two megalodon teeth from a depth of over 14,000 feet, hauling them from the manganese dioxide-rich red clay deposit on the seabed. In 1959, these were examined by Russian scientist Dr. W. Tschernezky, who investigated the thickness of the manganese dioxide layer deposited over them.

Knowing the rate at which such deposits form over time, Tschernezky was able to state that one of the teeth was not more than 24,000 years old, and the other was little more than 11,000 years old. This meant that contrary to previous assumptions, megalodon was still alive as recently as the end of the Pleistocene period. Following on from this, is it possible that it could have persisted a further 11,000 years (a brief moment in geological terms) and still survive today?

It is hardly likely that a creature of megalodon's forty-three to fifty-five foot magnitude could survive undetected in modern times if it was a habitual surface dweller. However, if it resided primarily at greater depths and entered shallow waters infrequently, its probability of anonymity would be much greater.

Indeed, at the 1988 International Society of Cryptozoology Conference, California University shark specialist Dr. Eugenie Clark presented an entire paper examining the possibility of unknown species of shark still evading formal discovery within the virtually impenetrable reaches of the oceans' Stygian depths. Moreover, megalodon's huge food requirements could he readily satisfied at such depths hecause they are home to the equally spectacular giant squids, already known to be preyed upon by sperm whales. Why not by giant shark, too?

Finally, it should he noted that there are a numher of compelling eyewitness accounts on record, some given by experienced trawlers and other observers well versed in shark form and identity, which tell of rare encounters with frighteningly large sharks that resemble great whites in general shape and appearance but which seem to have been two to three times as long. Based upon fossil evidence, paleontologists consider that megalodon was much the same in general form and build as the great white, differing principally in absolute length. Could the sharks featured in these eyewitness accounts by reliable witensses have been modern-day megalodons?

Probably the most amazing of those accounts was given by the aforementioned fish specialist Dr. David G. Stead in *Sharks and Rays of Australian Waters*, which had been narrated to him in 1918 by some fishermen at Port Stephens, New South Wales. They told him that their series of heavily weighted crayfish pots had been carried away once by a ghostly, white shark so extraordinarily immense that they estimated its length to have been anything between 115 and 300 feet! Naturally, shock and surprise will distort estimation of length. However, even if we allow a very generous degree of exaggeration inspired by their sight of this awesome Moby Dick of the shark world, its length must still have been inordinately great. It seems highly unlikely that a sighting of a normal great white, which is a fairly common species in this area, would have exerted such an effect upon their judgment.

In Stead's view, they had encountered a living megalodon. Added to this is his own observation of some five-inch-long teeth resembling those of great whites which had been dredged up from the Pacific. In contrast to those of megalodon currently known to paleontologlsts, these were not fossilized!

It is a very sobering thought that the largest carnivorous shark which ever existed might still be alive. True, megalodon may not have attained eighty feet in length, but even a mathematically miniaturized version reaching fifty feet or so is still a creature of nightmare—effortlessly dwarfing the marauding manmade movie sharks to emphasize that even the most grandiose and grotesque outpourings of humanity's imagination cannot compete with the raw reality of nature.

Giant Jellyfish

Dr. Karl P. N. Shuker

March 1994

When the ship's bow emerged, the crew was horrified to perceive a colossal jellyfish, weighing at least twenty tons, draped all over its front.

Speculation about the existence of undiscovered sea monsters traditionally concentrates totally on sea serpents, giant octopuses, and ultra-giant squids. However, there is an additional, separate category—one invariably overlooked during such considerations, yet whose members might well comprise the most dangerous mystery beasts in the world.

One of the most bizarre foes faced by Sir Arthur Conan Doyle's fictional detective Sherlock Holmes is featured in a short story titled *The Adventure of the Lion's Mane*—in which Holmes describes an encounter, along a stretch of shingle in Sussex, as follows:

> I had reached the deepest and stillest pool when my eyes caught that for which they were searching, and I burst into a shout of triumph.
>
> "Cyanea!" I cried. "Cyanea. Behold the Lion's Mane!"
>
> The strange object at which I pointed did indeed look like a tangled mass torn from the mane of a lion. It lay upon a rocky shelf some three feet under the water, a curious, waving, vibrating, hairy creature with streaks of silver among its yellow tresses. It pulsated with a slow, heavy dilation and contraction.
>
> "It has done mischief enough. Its day is over!" I cried. "Help me Stackhurst! Let us end the murderer forever."
>
> There was a big boulder just above the ledge, and we pushed it until it fell with a tremendous splash into the water. When the ripples had cleared we saw that it had settled upon the ledge below. One flapping edge of yellow membrane showed that our victim was beneath it. A thick oily scum oozed out from below the stone and stained the water round, rising slowly to the surface.

The creature in question, reponsible in the story for the death of a schoolmaster, was *Cyanea capillata*, the lion's mane jellyfish, whose Arctic form is the world's largest known type of jellyfish. One immense specimen, recorded from Massachusetts Bay in 1865, had a bell diameter of over seven feet and gigantic tentacles stretching 120 feet, yielding a tentacle spread of about 245 feet. Bearing in mind that each such jellyfish has numerous tentacles which are ringed by thousands of stinging and paralyzing cells called nematocysts, contact with such a monster by an unwary swimmer could prove extremely dangerous.

As yet, no human fatality has been formally recorded with this particular type (except for Sherlock Holmes' account). But there are smaller species whose nematocyst toxin is much more potent, and for which human fatalities have indeed been confirmed. The most notorious of these killers is Flecker's sea wasp *Chironex fleckeri* from Australia, whose sting is so agonizing that it is claimed to be the most excruciating pain known to humans. Some of its victims have died in convulsions of screaming insanity caused by the unrelenting agony induced by the briefest of skin contact with its tentacles' nematocysts.

Remarkably, this terrible creature remained completely unknown to science until 1956. But even more astounding is the likelihood that in the depths of the sea are still-unknown giant jellyfish whose stings could well rival those of *Chironex*. This possibility is raised by various little-publicized eyewitness accounts, which are now brought together here for cryptozoological investigation for the first time.

One of the most dramatic cases on record was documented by James Sweeney in *Sea Monsters*, and took place in January 1973. While sailing toward the Fiji Islands from Australia, the 1,483-ton vessel *Kuranda* encountered very turbulent waves, and while navigating through them the front portion of the ship dipped down into the water and seemed to collide with something beneath the surface. When the ship's bow emerged, the crew was horrified to perceive a colossal jellyfish, weighing at least twenty tons, draped all over its front.

A Monstrous, Animated Blob

The object the ship had collided into, this mostrous animated glob thrashed enormously long tentacles across the deck. To terrified eyewitnesses it must have resembled a disembodied gorgon's head with countless serpents for hair lashing out with venomous intent in all directions. An unfortunate crew member came within range of those deadly tentacles, which adhered to his skin. He was pulled clear by other seamen on board, but the tentacles had seared into his flesh so severely that, according to one eyewitness, he looked as if he had been scalded by steam.

And as if the danger posed by this creature's tentacles were not enough, an additional threat was conferred by virtue of its colossal bulk—which seemed likely to send the *Kuranda* plunging down to the sea bottom. According to the *Kuranda*'s captain, Langley Smith, the deck was awash in a two-feet-deep mass of tentacular slime, and some of the tentacles themselves were estimated to be at least 200 feet long.

Frantically, the crew did their best to clear the deck of this gelatinous horror, but its formidable stinging capability deterred every attempt made. If they needed any further proof of its deadly potency, the seaman who had been stung earlier had since died from his injuries.

This frightening episode could well have ended in tragedy, but happily an SOS put out by the *Kuranda* was detected by the *Hercules*, a deep-sea salvage tug 500 miles away, which set out at once to offer whatever assistance it could. The dreadful sight of the stupendous jellyfish enveloping a sizable portion of the *Kuranda* met the near-unbelieving eyes of the *Hercules* crew when they drew near, but with the aid of two high-pressure hoses spraying steam directly at the creature, it was eventually dislodged.

Following the *Kuranda*'s arrival back in Sydney, samples of the jellyfish's gelatinous slime were formally analyzed, and the specimen they were derived from was tentatively identified as a lion's mane—but one of incomparably huge proportions.

Another immense (but seemingly less belligerent) jellyfish monster had come to notice three years earlier. In November 1969, skin divers Richard Winer and Pat Boatwright encountered an almost round, gigantic object pulsating beneath them at a depth of 100 to 150 feet, while they were diving in waters fourteen miles southwest of Bermuda. As reported by Gary Mangiacopra (*Of Sea and Shore*, Fall 1976), the mysterious entity had a diameter of 50-100 feet, and was deep purple in color, with a pink-shaded outer rim. As they observed it, the creature slowly drifted up through the water toward them, inducing the divers to begin their own ascent with all speed, whereupon their pursuer paused, and then began descending once more.

Who Eats the Sharks?

What must surely be the most controversial giant jellyfish case on file featured one such monster's supposed engulfing of the two children and wife of French fisherman Henri Baiselle. He claims the monster struck while they were swimming with him in the sea near Bordeaux during the late 1980s.

Not too surprisingly, Baiselle's account of a huge jellyfish the size of a car that swallowed up his family before sinking out of sight failed to prevent the local police from arresting him on a murder charge, but he passed a lie-detector test and refused to change his story (*Fortean Times*, Fall 1990).

So far, the jellyfish reported have been fairly typical in shape, if not in size, but there is one very macabre mystery beast on record that may well be a scientifically unknown repesentative of one of their more specialized, deep sea forms. This is the singularly eerie creature spied by a diver in the South Pacific sometime prior to the mid-1950s. As revealed by Eric Frank Russell in his book *Great World Mysteries*, the diver had been following a shark, and was resting on the edge of a chasm leading down to much deeper depths, still watching the shark, when an immense, dull-brown, shapeless mass rose up out of the chasm, pulsating sluggishly, and generally flat in outline with ragged edges.

It was apparently devoid of eyes or other instantly recognizable sensory organs, but despite this it evidently discerned the shark's presence somehow, because it floated up until its upper surface made direct contact. The shark instantly gave a convulsive shudder and was then drawn without resistance into the hideous monster's body. The creature then sank back down into the chasm, leaving behind a very frightened diver to ponder what might have happened if that nightmarish, nameless entity had not been attracted to the shark!

In the past, a deep sea octopus has been suggested as a possible identity for this disturbing creature, but in reality a deep sea jellyfish is a much more plausible candidate. To begin with, all octopuses have tentacles, but a number of jellyfish (including known deep sea species) do not. However, all jellyfish are armed with nematocysts (sometimes on their body surface as well as on their tentacles), which in some species, as noted earlier, can elicit paralysis or indescribable pain. Accordingly, if the amorphous creature observed by the diver was equipped with a plentiful supply of these, the immediate paralysis of the shark could be readily explained. Although the shark's killer lacked obvious sensory organs such as eyes (this is true of all jellyfish), its ability to detect the shark can again be explained via the jellyfish identity. These animals possess primitive sensory structures receptive to water movements. Hence the creature would have been able to detect the water disturbances created by the shark's swimming. How fortunate it was that, by choosing to watch the shark, the diver had remained stationary!

A Grotesque Sea Monster

Deep sea jellyfish that are similar, though not identical, to the above example may explain Chilean legends of a grotesque sea monster called the *hide*, documented by Jorge Luis Borges in his famous work, *The Book of Imaginary Beings*. According to Borges, the hide is an octopus that resembles in shape and size a cowhide stretched out flat, with countless eyes all around its body's perimeter, and four larger ones in the center. It lives by rising to the surface of the sea and swallowing any animals or people swimming there.

As this description makes no mention of tentacles, it seems highly unlikely that such a beast (assuming that it really does exist) could be any form of octopus. In any event, octopuses only have a single pair of eyes, not a whole series around the edge of their body and two pairs of principal eyes. Conversely, many jellyfish possess peripheral sensory organs called rhopalia, which incorporate simple, light-sensitive eyespots or ocelli.

Moreover, although no jellyfish has true eyes, some—such as the common moon jellyfish *Aurelia aurita*—have four deceptively eye-like organs visible in the center of their bell (which are actually portions of their gut, known as gastric pouches. In short, a jellyfish candidate provides a far more realistic answer to the question of the hide's identity than an octopus does.

It is very possible that jellyfish notably larger than any yet recorded by science do exist in our world's vast oceans. Most may well exist in the abyssal depths, where humans at present have scarcely begun to penetrate.

It would seem that we will only learn more about these least-known of sea monsters—monsters that might conceivably be the most dangerous mystery beasts in the world—when they themselves choose to make their presence felt.

Giant Squids on the Attack

Michael Goss
August 1985

As onlookers watched in horror, the enraged sea creature wrapped its monstrous tentacles around the ship.

For centuries tales have been told of giant squids attacking ships and sailors. But until 1861, when the French ship Alecton encountered and tried to capture one, zoologists considered the giant squid (known as the *kraken* in Scandinavian mythology) to be no more real a denizen on the deep than the mermaid. A specimen caught in Newfoundland in 1873 and measuring fifty-five feet from tail to tentacle tip is the largest recognized by science but several authorities believe some squids may grow to four times that size.

Stories of aggressive behavior by giant squids usually turn out to be exaggerated or fictional. One puzzling case, however, may be an exception. In 1941, after a German raider sank the troopship he was on, Lieutenant. R. E. G. Cox saw—or so he claimed—a giant squid snatch one of his fellow survivors. Soon afterwards Cox felt a probing tentacle affix itself to his leg. He carried the scars for the rest of his life; they were sufficiently impressive to persuade biologist John L. Cloudsley-Thompson of the truth of his story. But in the end the contradictions in Cox's various versions of the experience make the case less than satisfactory.

Let us now consider the story of the *Pearl*, said to have been engulfed by a kraken in the Bay of Bengal on May 10, 1874.

The item was sent by an anonymous correspondent to *The London Times*—not a newspaper given to printing known or conjectured hoaxes—where it appeared on July 4, 1874, under the Shipping News column as "A Successor to the Sea Serpent." It opens with the steamer *Strathowen* bound past the southern tip of Ceylon on course for Madras. An hour before sunset on May 10, 1874, she sighted a schooner becalmed; it was the 150-ton *Pearl*. As he watched through binoculars, the writer saw between the two ships (but a little closer to the *Pearl*) "a long, low swelling lying on the sea, which from its color and shape I took to be a bank of seaweed."

Suddenly this mass moved forward, hitting the *Pearl* so forcefully that she reeled and swayed sideways. The watcher, now one of several, saw "the enormous mass and the hull . . . coalescing." Gradually her masts came lower and the ship lay on her beam-ends. Moments later she was gone and the race was on to reach the survivors visible struggling in the waves.

Among the survivors was the ship's master James Floyd whose account details how the *Pearl* was grappled and overwhelmed by a "gigantic cuttlefish or calamary." He supplies data on the ship's cargo, destination, and even her position in brisk, prosaic style as befits a seaman—until the point at which he and members of the six-man crew begin to discuss the nature of the brownish mass that had risen out of the sea on the ship's port side. Thereupon his style undergoes a transformation and starts to read like a nautical-fiction writer's attempt at character-dialogue. (For instance, one character says, "And it ain't the sea sarpent . . . for he's too round for that ere crittur.") The reader gets the distinct impression that a sober record of fact has abruptly given way to a yarn of the salt seas.

Floyd decided no harm would be done if he squeezed off a shot at the mystery object. ("Have a care, master; that ere is a squid," Bill Darling warns solemnly, "and will capsize us if you hurt him." The writer adds that Bill was a Newfoundlander, as if that fact alone deserved some kind of respect in this context. Maybe it does.) The shot caused the monster to shake and seconds later men were following Bill Darling's desperately shouted advice to break out knives and axes as the vast body with its "train" about 100 feet long surged forward to strike the *Pearl* a shuddering blow. They were too late.

"Monstrous arms like trees" caused the small ship to keel over as the squid squeezed on board, using its huge body weight to bring the ship onto its beam-ends. Floyd's last memory was of a man squashed between one of the huge arms and a mast; the next moment he was in the water. The real-life kraken carried below with it the *Pearl* and two of her crew members, Tom Fielding and Bill.

Or did it? From Edward Newman (editor of *The Zoologist*) in 1874 to Bernard Heuvelmans almost a century later, those who have looked closely at the *Pearl* story have been less than happy with it—as a record of straight fact, that is. Less caring writers, though, have uncritically rehashed Frank Lane's retelling of the episode in his influential *Kingdom of the Octopus*, without noting Lane's reservations. Lane was disturbed that the names of the ships and seamen could not be verified in period maritime sources. Yet certain internal evidence within the narrative led him to believe it was at least possible that the story was true.

His research spotlighted some modern reports of large squids behaving in ways that mimicked those of the 1874 "cuttle" fairly closely. Sailing between Hawaii and Samoa from 1930 to 1933, the 15,000-ton Norwegian tanker *Brunswick* was attacked no fewer than three times. No squid could make an impression against the smooth steel hull of the tanker but on a wooden hull such as that of the diminuitive *Pearl*, the results might have been quite different. Here at least we have some evidence that giant squids may be temperamentally capable of assaulting vessels far larger than the *Pearl*. Captain Floyd had testified that his schooner was in ballast at the time of the attack. As ballast shifted under the lurching efforts of the cephalopod it might have created the critical momentum that capsized the small craft. (Otherwise we'd hardly expect even the largest squid to possess the purchase to make the feat possible.)

"To me the most convincing evidence is that the man who issues the warning to the master, Bill Darling, was a Newfoundlander," Lane writes. "At the time of this incident the one place in the world where men were most likely to know about large squids and their ferocity if attacked was Newfoundland."

It is true that in 1874 Newfoundlanders had a certain advantage over others when it came to knowledge of these rarely found cephalopods; a number of spectacular specimens had been stranded off the shores of Newfoundland. By putting a warning into the mouth of a Newfoundland sailor, then, the writer adds—or intends to add—a further touch of veracity to the story.

Lane makes the case that by May 1874, the date at which the story is set, details of the stranded Newfoundland giants would not have reached India, where the story allegedly originated. A hoaxer ignorant of these specimens would have no reason to connect Newfoundland with the giant squid or to make Bill Darling a native of that island.

Lane's reasoning seems logical on the surface. But a skeptic could retort that the presence of Bill Darling indicates that details of the Newfoundland strandings not only could have reached India but most definitely *had* done so. More than that, the existence of Darling could have been an open invitation for discerning readers to see through the hoax by identifying the material on which it drew for inspiration. One who evidently glimpsed the "Newfoundland connection" was *Zoologist* editor Newman; but beyond noting a possible desire on the part of somebody "to burlesque and discredit the American [sic] narratives," he drew back from making an outright accusation.

Had he probed deeper, Newman might have had his suspicions reinforced by one important incident within the *Pearl* story. The giant stirred into violent action as a result of being attacked (somewhat gratuitously) is notably close to the reaction of the specimen met in Conception Bay, Newfoundland, on October 26, 1873; this encounter was well known and well publicized in major zoological journals. *The Field* (December 13, 1873, or January 31, 1874), the *Proceedings of the Zoological Society of London* (March 3, 1874) or the *Annals & Magazine of Natural History* (January 1874) all reproduced details of descriptions given by Reverand Moses Harvey not long after the squid was seen.

Yet beyond giving a certain topicality to the theme of the story—and explaining the inclusion of Bill Darling, the squid-wise Newfoundlander—these papers may have been an unnecessary luxury for our hypothetical hoaxer. He had only to rework Pierre Denys de Montfort's perennially-cited vintage tale of the heroic St. Malo mariners chopping away as the monster draws their vessel ever closer to the waves and to destruction. The situation in the *Pearl* story is identical.

Communications between Britain and India at this time were reasonably good—good enough for the proposed hoaxer to have received news of the Newfoundland squid strandings, to have come up with a fictitious account dating from May and to have got it to *The Times* for its appearance on July 4. (On July 31, incidentally, a Connecticut newspaper carried a truncated version of the same report.) Besides an efficient mailboat service—a London-Bombay P&O ship would take on average three weeks for the journey—news items regularly passed across a popular telegraphy link between the two countries; one experiment showed it was quicker by just over two hours to send a telegram from Madras to London than from Calcutta to Madras.

The flow of news between these two countries casts a further, final doubt on the *Pearl* incident. English readers were supposedly getting a story that had already been sent to the Indian papers; yet scanning the *Times of India* for May and June 1874, one finds no mention of this newsworthy event—despite that paper's sustained interest in shipping reports and sharp eye for derisory items in rival Indian publications.

None of these objections absolutely proves the sinking of the *Pearl* to have been a hoax. But taken together they strongly indicate that the story is very, very suspect.

So it appears that the kraken, its fierce reputation to the contrary, is not the terror of the sea. But it remains one of the sea's most awesome inhabitants and one of its deepest mysteries.

Bermuda Triangle Mysteries

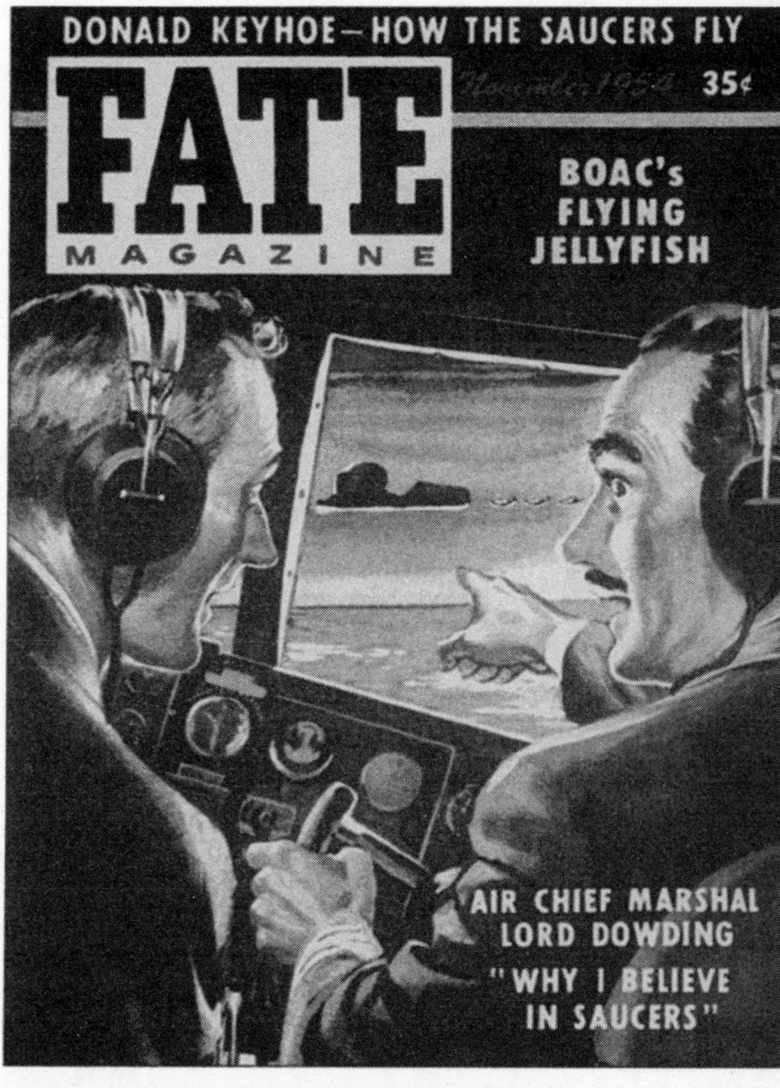

The Triangle with Four (or More) Sides

Martin Caidin

January 1993

We're talking about a half-million square miles of ocean that's a trapezium—a rectangle in which no two sides or angles are the same. It's a skewed rectangle, and it derives its ominous reputation from hard numbers.

It all depends on what you're reading. Sometimes it's called the Bermuda Triangle. But if the writer selects on the basis of a more commanding and grisly effect, the words shift to become the Devil's Triangle. It's also known as the Devil's Graveyard and a host of other titles, which mercifully we will put aside.

All the names point to that area of the Atlantic Ocean infamous for a staggering loss—often without any trace of ships, planes, and people. Most books and articles on the Bermuda Triangle (the name may be less esoteric but at least we're not pounding it for effect) are inordinately fond of reproducing a map, or perhaps a satellite photo of that ocean area, with a dramatically heavy line that runs from the island of Bermuda straight down to Key West, doodles off to somewhere in Cuba or Puerto Rico, and then shoots back northward to Bermuda.

But that's not the way it is. Oh, there's a specific area, all right, but it's difficult to find more than a few people who will agree on just what is that area. Even those of us who've flown through the Bermuda Triangle, and sailed it as well, find it necessary at times to alter the sides of the triangle because of some new event or disappearance that adds another bit of hard data to the Legend-That's-True.

We're talking about a half-million square miles of ocean that's a trapezium—a rectangle in which no two sides or angles are the same. It's a skewed rectangle, and it derives its ominous reputation from hard numbers.

In the thirty years from 1945 through 1975, sixty-seven ships and boats of all sizes, and at least 192 aircraft (there are more but exact proof is lacking) of all types, involving nearly 1,700 human beings, have vanished within the Bermuda Triangle without a shred of evidence to explain their loss.

Not a word of what you have just read is conjecture, or bending a single fact, or assuming anything. It is simply the truth, a bitter and often frightening reality. The why of those disappearances is where the shouting and name-calling begins, but, hold on just a moment until we better define what this writer, pilot, and seaman defines a bit more carefully as the Triangle.

Convenient as it may be to start defining the area by stabbing a pencil on the chart dot called Bermuda, that would be too specific without justification. Take the area of Bermuda, one or two hundred miles in all directions from that island (and other smaller islands), and then draw a wide band to Wilmington/North Myrtle Beach in North Carolina. From this area, make another wide swath generally southward, but taking in the entire coastline right on down to an area perhaps a hundred miles south of Key West. Continue southeast, still with that wide swath, to Puerto Rico, and then bend around to a generally northeast direction back to Bermuda. You may have a rectangle with four unequal sides or something that seems to have five sides, but you're just as accurate if you draw on that chart a huge lopsided ink blot that takes in the same general area.

I've taken this time for specifying the area itself to avoid the urge of so many to create a charted triangle to lend credence to the shape. The shape doesn't mean a thing, it's the area within from which ships and planes have vanished without leaving any sign of what caused them to disappear. If you utilize this shape and area then you'll discover the sixty-seven ships and 192 planes are somewhat fewer than the actual number of disappearances.

In any attempt to learn what caused these mysterious and frustrating losses of ships, aircraft and people, there's a natural, almost urgent, need to blame the shape of the area involved, and that is extremely misleading. It doesn't supply any answers, and to be blunt about it—you're dealing with a cop-out. Questions with possible answers, but to date nothing specific.

I stated that the sixty-seven ships and 192 aircraft are not the total number. Many aircraft flying along the American

East Coast or down through the islands that take us, in our "chart swath," to Puerto Rico before bending northeast back to Bermuda have never gone into the record books. Pilots often fly into this area without filing a flight plan or leaving any other evidence of their intended route. Others get caught in weather and end up far from shore in the Triangle.

Many military aircraft on missions that have been classified for one reason or another are never identified. You can count on perhaps hundreds or even thousands of fingers the drug runners, the illegal entry of aliens, the gun runners, the escapees from many island countries trying to reach the American mainland who have sailed or flown to nameless oblivion in this area.

Before even starting to try to understand how and why there has been such a stupendous loss of life without even a trace of such losses, let me make a point that in the name of accuracy and common sense. Many thousands of sea voyages have been made through the Bermuda Triangle in absolute safety, peace and harmony—and you can add whatever adjectives you wish to those trips.

Just as there have been hundreds of thousands of flights of aircraft through the Triangle without even the cough of an engine or the unexplained twitch of an instrument dial. That issue must be stated clearly, lest the reader judge that launching into the Triangle assures one of fright or mystery "just because you're there." After all, airliners have been flying through that area for decades in absolute safety

But not all of them, and that also is the issue at hand. The loss of several hundred ships and aircraft is no small matter, and one must be weighed against the other.

For the record, and that is important for the reader, I've been flying in the area we identify as the Bermuda Triangle for decades. Literally. This includes aircraft beginning with the diminutive Piper TriPacer and Cessna 172, and then scaling upward to the Piper Apache, Piper Aztec, Beech Twin Bonanza (I ran a small charter airline with a few of these operating out of Florida), Cessna 310, Piper Comanche and Twin Comanche, the Douglas C-47 and its civilian equal, the DC-3. I've gone through this same area in the Douglas C-118 (military version of the DC-6B), the Lockheed C-130 Hercules, the Consolidated PBY-6A Catalina, and, well, there are others, but I believe the point is made. I've made the flights in perfect weather (severe clear) and I've been out there in a violent hurricane, on a search mission for a downed airliner (at least we judge it was downed; it vanished with all aboard).

Heart of the Matter

Our interest is not in the flights made without incident, for those are like any other flights to other destinations. Nor am I going to refer to the flights of pilot friends who went through eerie and frightening moments and were deeply grateful for surviving a flight they believed was their last. As sincere and accurate as such flights may be, that is secondary information, and our concern is with firsthand experience. No intermediaries.

The incident at hand is real, detailed, recorded, and witnessed beyond even the most tenuous shred of doubt. There may be, and likely there will be, naysayers in the reading audience. Little matter. This is a moment of reality and it matters not one whit what somebody who wasn't there may have in the way of comment. At its best, it is armchair pontificating; at worst it's just someone babbling about something they know next to nothing about.

The aircraft is a Consolidated PBY-6A Catalina; this particular model was manufactured under license in Canada. It is a large flying boat that performed yeoman service before, during, and after World War II. This particular "Cat" is the property of Connie Edwards of Big Spring, Texas, and carries the FAA identification (registration) of N4C.

On the June 11, 1986, we neared the conclusion of a flight that had taken the flying boat from Texas into Canada, to and through the Azores, into Lisbon, Portugal, then northward to Santiago, Spain, and farther northward to land in Plymouth Harbor in southern England. Later we flew on to Yeovilton, the British base for its Fleet Air Arm, before starting the return flight from England back to the Azores, and then a flight (into strong headwinds) from Lajes in the Azores to Bermuda that took us more than twenty-two hours of nonstop flying.

The last leg of me and my wife, Dee Dee, who is also a pilot, was from Bermuda to Jacksonville Naval Air Station on the northeast coastline of Florida. Among the people in the Catalina for this run were myself and Dee Dee; Connie Edwards of incredible flying experience and skill; Randy Sohn, an airline captain who also is qualified to fly any piston-engined warbird built anywhere in the world; USN Captain Art Ward, probably the leading instrument pilot of the entire U.S. Navy; Al Brown, veteran Air Force flight engineer, mechanic, and pilot; and, the youngest of the lot, Connie's son, Tex Edwards, who in his teens was rated for everything from single-engine planes to four-engine transports or bombers. Understand the importance of these names: veteran, experienced, skilled, ability-recognized pilots who'd flown through, over, and around most of the world.

Just as germane to the flight were the instrumentation and avionics (flight electronics) we had aboard this airplane. We're talking about a considerable fortune in equipment. Aside from the two-of-everything of instruments, Connie and Al Brown packed into this airplane a radar altimeter, an HF radio, VLF Omega, and other navigational equipment. Then he added more radios and navigation gear, including a second Loran C (device to pinpoint locations using information from overhead satellites), two more ADFs, another encoding altimeter and—well, put it this way: our radar altimeters measured the waves beneath us down to the accuracy of one foot. Our navigation systems would let us know—anywhere in the world—if we were so much as a tenth of a mile off the planned course.

We communicated by satellite links with any spot in the world. We had a system that let us link up to a weather satcom at 22,300 miles so that we were fed printouts of photographs taken from space of where we were flying at that moment, and you can't get better weather checking than that!

We had equipment in that airplane that not too many years before this flight was a dream—not yet available—for pilots. We also had more powerful engines that went into this bird, and we had two huge fuel tanks slung beneath the wings (longer than the wings of a B-17 bomber) so that we could fly at least twenty-eight to thirty hours nonstop.

We enjoyed the satellite photo printouts. They showed the only clouds far south of us, a line that curved southward and then westward from Bermuda to the Melbourne area. The nearest clouds to us once we were on our way would be at least 200 miles south of us.

On the morning of June 11, 1986, in perfect, warm, balmy weather we set course for JAX Naval Air Station. You could see just about forever. Few flights were set up as well as this with the skies clear, two purring powerful engines, a grand flying machine with great inherent stability, the safety of being able to land on the ocean if that ever became our need, and an array of electronics that gave us a running account of our position about as close as you can get to a gnat's eyelash. Beautiful; that was the word.

Those pilots who decided to "sit this one out" and let the others fly gathered in the aft compartment between the two big gun blisters where leather couches and pillows had replaced the .50 caliber machine guns. After a few hours in the air, my wife went forward to take the left seat—the position for pilot-in-command. It was great hand-flying, which means you had to fly hands-on. Despite all the super electronic gizmos on board, the PBY didn't have an autopilot, which is just the way Connie Edwards wanted his airplane. You were up there to fly. But it was calm flying. Pay attention to where the needles and numbers on the gauges pointed, and fly her with a gentle hand. The PBY is like a whale, and everything seems to take place in slow motion.

Then it happened. I was up front in the cockpit, standing behind and between the two pilot seats. I watched idly through the side windows at groups of dolphins beneath us, and every now and then we'd pass a sailing ship or a seagoing yacht. I shifted my gaze from the right side of the airplane to the left, and had the left wing, all the way out to the wing tip (wingspan is 110 feet), in sight.

Disappearing Act

It disappeared. I blinked. Nothing seemed to have changed. The engines thundered smoothly, the propellers synchronized, the great flying boat steady as a rock. But I couldn't see the outer portion of the left wing. A pilot's first thought, of course, is that we'd flown into a cloud, or a fog, or even some crazy mist that was heaving up to 4,000 feet. But a few moments before moving forward to the cockpit I had checked the metsat photos beamed down from space, and there wasn't a smidgin of cloud or anything else within 200 miles of us.

I turned to look at the right wing, and in that movement my vision moved through the field of view of the cockpit looking forward. I saw the nose clearly and remembered how starkly the cleat in nose center (for mooring) stood out clearly. Beyond the airplane nose there was nothing.

What in the hell was this? I snapped a look out to the right window and the right wing simply disappeared from sight! It was an eerie feeling, as though we'd flown into some impossible limbo. I took careful stock of everything about me, and then noticed that what had been blue sky had also changed color. A creamy yellow, as though we were in the middle of a bottle of eggnog. I looked around in all directions.

We seemed to be suspended in an infinity of murky yellow. If we couldn't check the instruments, there was no way to know we were flying at just over 100 mile per hour—as we saw on the ASI (air-speed indicator). And looking at the instrument panel was enough to chill anyone's blood down to the freezing level.

A pilot depends on his (or her) instruments for balancing, maneuvering, and navigating when flying in IMC (Instrument Meteorological Conditions), and sure as winter follows summer we were in IMC! But the instruments so important to us were going crazy, and few things will raise the hackles along the back of your neck than the sight of those gauges and instruments going belly up.

Because there wasn't any more hint of why they were failing than there was for the world outside the airplane to dissolve into that creamy yellow murk, what was strange became stranger. We looked in every direction from the airplane.

We were surprised to see we had a narrow-diameter "hole" through which we could look straight up to see blue sky, and, if we looked straight down, through this same small-diameter space there was the ocean. It was as if a long pipe extended from the surface to the sky above, providing this keyhole of vision, and the pipe sped along with the airplane.

The first sign of something wrong with the gauges was picked up by Dee Dee, since she was in the left seat and scanning the gauges as part of her flying. We didn't need the magnetic compass with all our super avionics, but the damn thing is supposed to perform in a reliable manner. Ours began to swing back and forth and quickly went into a blur of movement as it whirled crazily in its bath of alcohol.

Moments later the DG (the Directional Gyro that supplies a gyroscopic heading to follow) played catchup with the mag compass, and began its own wild (and useless) swinging. As fast as we could move our gaze from one instrument to another, they were failing. The artificial horizon—gyroscopic representation of the horizon and the world outside the airplane—fell over like a punctured chicken and wobbled as if demented.

And then the real trouble started. We had a zillion bucks worth of super electronics in this airplane, and abruptly they began to fall over as if paralyzed. Two million dollars of avionics just up and died. We didn't know what in the hell was wrong other than just about everything in that airplane, save the barometric-pressure gauges, was gone. The LORAN was useless. Even the electronic fuel gauges, showing rate of flow and quantity, fluttered and blinked and became erratic, which is the same as worthless. Our intricate navigation gear blinked a few times and then every dial read 8888888888. Then the radios went dead!

Now, everything electronic was still being fed power from the aircraft electrical system. All power flow was normal, but none of it worked anymore. It was as if everything electronic had gone into a coma. We couldn't see even the wingtips, we had no navigation, the most rudimentary of gauges—the mag compass—had become a whirling dervish, and Dee Dee continued to fly by aiming at the brightest area of the horizon, which meant westward. We took turns in the right seat or standing behind the pilot seats, "riding shotgun" on each other.

We were flying now by the most rudimentary systems—airspeed, altitude, rate of climb or descent, and a turn-slip-skid indicator that operated like a seal balancing a ball on its nose and functioned without outside power, and that was it. This was the way pilots flew only a dozen years after the Wright Brothers took to the air!

But that's all we had. We had no idea of what had cut our equipment down to junk. The engines roared perfectly, the airplane flew with that solid Catalina feel, but we were no longer in any world we knew. We figured if it was crazy up high, let's go down—by studying the waves through that peephole of looking straight down, and also counting (but not too much) on the altimeter. We dropped down to perhaps 20 or 30 feet off the water, but we couldn't see forward any distance greater than that. "We're gonna run into a damn ship down this low," someone offered, and immediately we went back to altitude.

Still that same gummy yellow gunk all about us. If I ever wanted to know what it's like to drift through limbo where the dominant hue is creamy eggnog, I've now experienced this. After a while, out of touch with the rest of the planet, we began exchanging pilots in the left seat. Young Tex took over for a while and Art Ward stayed up front with him, with Al Brown studying everything from behind them.

I wasn't flying this leg, so I went back with Dee Dee to the gun blisters where we might as well have been in some luxury salon. That was another crazy part about all this. No matter that what we were in—trapped is as good a word as any—no one in the airplane reacted as if there were any danger. Hell, with two exceptions (Dee Dee and Tex), the rest of us had been flying all our lives and we'd had a few memorable experiences. The calm of the pilots would have astounded anyone not familiar with this background. We were here, it was impossible, the airplane was still flying—so, keep flying.

Connie Edwards and Randy Sohn went forward to take the controls. About ninety minutes (estimated by clock time) out of JAX, we seemed to penetrate an invisible curtain. Imagine you're up there in this soup with us. For hours the only world is eggnog and that ridiculous periscope view of straight up or down, and the most advanced flight electronic systems in the world are as dead as dodos.

Then suddenly you're flying in perfect, crystal clean, clear air. No more eggnog. We swung into a wide turn to see where we had been. The sky was absolutely clear behind us as far as we could see. Whatever had enveloped us for hours was gone.

"Hey, we're coming back on line!" came the word. The artificial horizon revived itself, the directional gyro steadied down and the mag compass quivered gently. The rows of 8888888888 blurred away and the proper numbers began to read out on radio, LORAN, transponder, radar altimeter and everything else. We could talk via satcom link to anywhere in the world. The ocean was clear beneath us, the sky above a bright blue. We passed an increasing number of ships, made contact with JAX NAS, saw we'd have to punch through some heavy rain showers (and they looked wonderful) and Connie set her down on the JAX runway like we had feathers beneath us.

For some four hours, what happened to us, as any sober scientist or engineer will tell you without a moment's hesitation, was and is absolutely impossible.

Of course, those scientists weren't up there with us, and so no matter how many sheepskins hang on their walls, they don't know what the hell they're talking about.

Let me conclude this with the wisdom of a great pilot and a great writer recently departed from this life, for no one ever said it better than did Ernest K. Gann in his magnificent book, *Fate Is the Hunter*. He said that no matter what the science or the engineering, no matter how thorough the planning, no matter how skilled the crews or exhaustive the preparations, airplanes will go down from causes unknown. And a pilot unskilled in instrument flight on this day of the yellow sky would never have survived those hours of limbo.

"Somewhere in the heavens," wrote Ernie Gann, "there is a great invisible genie who every so often lets down his pants and pisses all over the pillars of science."

Count on it.

No one has ever come forward with an acceptable explanation of the "yellow sky, as if flying in a bottle of eggnog," or how it suddenly appeared, or what it was. Neither is there any clearcut definition of why gyroscopic and magnetic instruments, which had worked perfectly for weeks of flying, suddenly spun uselessly. And there is even greater mystery as to why several million dollars worth of new electronics—always with power fed properly to them—became useless and ceased to function.

The single explanation that appears to make sense is that the Catalina flying boat was enveloped, or was affected by, an intense electromagnetic field that dumped the instruments and "blanked out" the electronic equipment. Where did it come from? No one knows. Or was it really an electromagnetic field? No one knows that either. But the point was made that any pilot caught in that "soup" who lacked experienced flying skills with basic instruments and no outside reference would almost certainly have lost control and crashed into the ocean. We add this item to this report. The erratic behavior of magnetic and gyroscopic instruments is uncommon, but it has been encountered by other aircraft and pilots. So has the "yellow sky" where all reference to the outside world vanishes.

The more experienced pilots have emerged from their travail. But not all, and we don't know how many fell victim to these bizarre conditions.

Eyewitness in the Bermuda Triangle

John Miller
January 1993

Andy Raymond will never forget his three years in the Bermuda Triangle. He needs no one to convince him of its terrible mystery, because he knows it's real.

Many investigators have written about the Bermuda Triangle from afar, but no description of that most enigmatic area of ocean can match the accounts of people who have actually lived there. One such person is Andy Raymond, a Chicago contract engineer, who made the Bermuda Triangle his home from 1979 to 1982. During that time, he was project manager for the "Island of Science," where professionally trained researchers experimented with solar power, the nutritional potential of seaweed, and an accelerated wind lab.

Under his direction were forty Bahamians and a dozen Haitians, who commuted daily from other nearby islands, while he resided on the Island of Science, with occasional flights to Great Harbor Cay, about thirty minutes away.

It was on these air commutes that the Bermuda Triangle phenomenon would often occur.

Most of his flights from the Island of Science were strictly routine, but during a few of them his magnetic compass would spin crazily, as though powered by an electric motor. For a man like Andy Raymond, such occurrences had to be the results of presently unknown but ultimately explainable natural forces.

He was familiar with most of the paranormal theories and stories about the Bermuda Triangle and dismissed them all out of hand as just plain malarkey. He is a no-nonsense construction engineer who knows how to party hardy with no room in between for wacko speculations. But one flight in particular was to open his mind and shake any rational explanation for unusual happenings in the Devil's Triangle.

July 5, 1980, a date he will remember the rest of his life, began as usual. It was one of those picture-postcard perfect days in south coastal Florida, with the sun shining out of an unobstructed sky on a mirror-smooth sea. Andy was along for a ride with his old friend, Howard Smith, a highly experienced bush pilot, who was returning a repaired clutch plate for a boat with motor problems in Grand Harbor, seventy nautical miles away. Smith's single-engine Cessna 172, call-letters 7-9-Tango, was loaded with some of the most advanced instrumentation available to civilian aviators. He had a costly DME (a sophisticated device for measuring the relationship of time and distance in flight), the latest in radio-direction finders, electric and magnetic compasses and a transponder. They arrived in Bimini without incident by noon, had a leisurely lunch, then took off into the same pristine weather conditions for Little Stirrup Cay, northernmost of the Bahamas and hardly more than an hour away.

Not long into their flight, however, they ran into a thick cloud cover and the sky grew suddenly dark. The array of instruments functioned perfectly. Both Smith and Andy had made this hop numerous times before, so neither had cause for concern, despite flying blind through the overcast.

When their DME informed them they had reached their destination, they dropped beneath the cloud cover to initiate their landing approach, but the scene that spread out before them belonged to another world or some alternate reality. Little Stirrup Cay was nowhere to be seen. Nor was there a sign of land anywhere in the otherwise island-bedecked part of the sea. No less awful was the eerie appearance of the water below them.

"It looked just like boiling copper," Andy recalled. "I have seen every kind of light effect the sun can bounce off the surface, but never anything even remotely approaching this." Moreover, the sun was hidden behind the thick overcast, while the waves roiled as though heated by some impossible submarine furnace, and glistened in a golden red fire that appeared to be generated from within the sea.

Smith got on the horn to Fort Lauderdale for assistance. The radio was dead. Flying too low now, he ascended into the darkening cloud cover again, trusting his instruments. Now they both could feel the strange tingling of electricity in the air. Moments later, the little Cessna suddenly plummeted 500 feet before Smith could restore control. Known as "micro-bursts" of air, they are powerful down-drafts within storm clouds. After the third or fourth occurrence, they descended beneath the clouds once more. The evil-looking copper-colored sea was gone, the sky suddenly cleared and before them was another private aircraft.

They followed it for a few minutes as it led them in a final approach to Grand Harbor, their point of origin. Incredibly, they were back where they started, even though they flew in a straight line in the opposite direction.

With the exception of their radio, the instruments had operated perfectly. Later, Smith calculated the time aloft to the distance covered and deduced that it would have been impossible to go out over open water as far as they did and round trip it back to Grand Harbor. Afterwards, Andy learned of firsthand accounts from friends in the U.S. Navy and Coast Guard of numerous, inexplicable disappearances made more mysterious by the fact that the area defined as the Bermuda Triangle is among the most thoroughly monitored quadrants on the globe. It is constantly eaves-dropped by the Bahama Air Service and Rescue, together with military and civilian radar and radio operators.

Theoretically, no serious trouble should occur without somebody taking notice. Andy himself survived two separate shipwrecks in the Bermuda Triangle and was rescued before he had a chance to get wet.

In the fall of 1981, he was involved in a baffling tragedy that still haunts him. It concerned two life-long robust friends in their sixties, who had grown up together in the Bahamas and understood those waters better than almost anyone. Their sailing expertise was well known, so when they filed their float plan to Palm Beach, no one doubted they could make the entirely routine cruise in under six hours. Even so, they were in regular ship-to-shore radio contact with their wives back at Grand Harbor Cay. They broadcast their position every thirty minutes on a high-powered single-band transmitter. The two old sea hands cast off at 9:00 a.m. under a windless, cloudless sky across a glass-smooth sea.

As promised, they radioed their precise location every half hour, describing the conditions through which they sailed as ideal. But when they failed to make their 1:00 p.m. transmission, their wives alerted the authorities. Within minutes, an armada of private, Coast Guard, and B.A.S.R. boats, including Andy Raymond, and a squadron of search aircraft swept the placid waters in all directions in a 200-mile radius of the fifty-eight-foot Hattaris yacht's last known position. The intensive search went on after nightfall and all the next day. Search efforts continued for another week before being called off. During all that time, the sea remained innocently calm. But it bore not a single trace of the vanished boat or its two accomplished seamen.

No oil slick, not even a single seat cushion—absolutely nothing was left behind. "I have seen all kinds of vessels, large and small, go down," Andy said. "Without exception, they all leave massive amounts of debris which survive their sinking by days. You would not believe the masses of material that cover the seas after a wreck. Even the smallest yacht belches enormous clouds of oil long after sinking. For a boat as big as the craft they sailed to go down and leave neither a huge oil slick nor a carpet of floating debris is impossible, especially considering the calm condition of the sea at that time."

Some days after the unsolved disappearance, Andy saw what he felt might be a clue to the deadly mystery of the Bermuda Triangle. While walking along the beach in water up to his knees, he came upon one of the Bahamas' famous

"Blue Holes." These represent a phenomenon not yet understood by oceanographers, but still being researched as the strangest feature of the Caribbean. They vary in diameter from a few feet to perhaps hundreds of yards, occur in shallow depths, contain water of a remarkably light blue color and go down, straight as a shaft, to immeasurable depths.

Exploring a Blue Hole about ten years ago, Jacques Cousteau photographed a perfectly preserved, turn-of-the-century rowboat sitting on a shelf about eighty feet down, as though carefully placed there by some mermaid who collected antique vessels.

Andy speculates these Blue Holes may go down to the very floor of the sea, where submarine earthquakes surge water pressure through them to generate sudden vortices. Appearing without warning for brief periods, they resemble a whirlpool like that created when the plug is pulled from a bathtub of water. The force they exert on the surface of the water is so great that anything within its vicinity is sucked without a trace to the bottom of the ocean, including aircraft, which are pulled into the vortex by down drafts similar to the micro-bursts Andy and Howard experienced in 1980. The atmospheric disturbances caused by such a vortex could account for the electromagnetic anomalies encountered in the immediate area of a disappearance.

Whatever the source of those disappearances, Andy Raymond will never forget his three years in the Bermuda Triangle. He needs no one to convince him of its terrible mystery, because he knows it is real.

The Hole in the Bermuda Triangle

C. J. Marrow

December 1985

What causes this anomaly? At present scientists can only conjecture. One of their most plausible theories is that sometime in the distant past, a large, heavy asteroid struck in this area.

One of the most mysterious and controversial areas in the world is that portion of the Atlantic Ocean bounded by Bermuda, the Bahamas and Florida known as the Bermuda Triangle. Actually, its boundaries are nebulous and arbitrary and it may well be more a circle than a triangle. Nevertheless, it has had an evil reputation for centuries—on which such authors as Charles Berlitz, John Wallace Spencer and Ivan Sanderson have not hesitated to capitalize. Despite more sober analyses, such as Larry Kusche's *The Bermuda Triangle Mystery—Solved*, diehard Triangle buffs insist that something happens there to down planes and ships. They may take heart from one satellite's findings in the late 1970s.

The sky—as we are all aware—is full of orbiting satellites doing a variety of jobs. Their acronyms are typical governmental jargon: GPS, Global Positioning System; GEOS, Geostationary Operational Environmental Satellites; LAGEOS, Laser Geodynamic Satellite, to name but a few. Since Sputnik was launched in 1957, some 14,000 pieces of hardware have been sent into space. Although many have fallen back, about 5,000 spacefarers are out there—some functioning, some not.

One-fourth of the satellites are in the service of science. Landsat, for instance, which went aloft with the shuttle *Columbia*, has mapped the entire earth, discovering dry river channels under Sahara Desert sands, cobbled streets in the Yucatan jungle and other significant data which help scientists track the development and history of our planet.

The oceanographic satellite *Seasat*, built at the Jet Propulsion Laboratory in Pasadena, California, and launched June 27, 1978, by the Atlas booster system, has mapped the seas. From its near-polar orbit the satellite observed the entire earth revolving beneath it. Further, a sun-synchronous orbit permitted the imaging satellite to take pictures with the sunlight always striking the earth at the same angle.

Seasat had five sensors functioning simultaneously, one of which—the radar altimeter—measured the distance between satellite and ocean surface to a precision of four inches. The surface of the sea, it develops, is not nearly as level as we have thought. Seasat mapped high and low ridges and troughs varying as much as 600 feet—not in the floor of the ocean, mind you, but on its surface. After a number of passes, the satellite equipment had recorded which variations were caused by currents, tides and storm surges and which were stationary surface measurements. Seasat accumulated much valuable data before a short circuit prematurely ended its mission in October 1978.

One of the most interesting and mysterious of Seasat's discoveries is a circular depression in the Atlantic Ocean just south of Bermuda—in short, in the Bermuda Triangle. This curious anomaly, shown distinctly on the Satellite Altimetric Sea Surface maps, is about twenty-five miles in diameter and fifty feet deep at its center. It is a round, permanent, consistent depression which shows no changes except for minor surface waves. It is not a whirlpool; it is stationary.

What causes this anomaly? At present scientists can only conjecture. One of their most plausible theories is that sometime in the distant past, a large, heavy asteroid struck in this area. Buried deep beneath the seafloor, its mass is more dense than the surrounding material so that it alters the earth's gravitational pull around its point of impact.

Is it possible that increased magnetic pull might contribute to the sudden development of unusual—and disastrous—weather conditions in the Triangle? More than 100 ships have been said to have foundered or disappeared there in the past 200 years. Allegedly, since the days of air travel, planes have vanished and pilots and navigators have frequently reported erratic compasses and malfunctioning equipment.

Whether the Bermuda Triangle is any more dangerous than any other part of the earth's vast seas is debatable. But it is a fact that Seasat found an anomalous circular depression there, which may or may not have something to do with the myths and legends that have flourished for centuries.

A letter written to FATE, from the large insurance firm Lloyd's of London, dated April 1, 1975, states, in part:

> According to Lloyd's Records, 428 vessels have been reported missing throughout the world since 1955, and it may interest you to know that our intelligence service can find no evidence to support the claim that the Bermuda Triangle has more losses than elsewhere. This finding is upheld by the United States Coast Guard whose computer-based records of casualties in the Atlantic go back to 1958.

Sea Mystery at Our Back Door

George X. Sand
October 1952

In this watery region off the coast of Florida ships and aircraft vanish without leaving a single clue.

The *Sandra* was a square-cut tramp steamer. Rust spots showed here and there along her 350-foot length. She carried twelve men and radio equipment. She had sailed from Savannah, Georgia, with 300 tons of insecticide destined for delivery at Puerto Cabello, Venezuela. It would not be delivered. Not ever!

Thumping her way leisurely southward through the heavily traveled steamer lanes off Jacksonville, the *Sandra* was on course. All was in order. From her bridge the friendly, winking beacon of St. Augustine Light must have been easily visible through the peaceful tropical dusk that shrouded the low Florida coastline off the starboard rail.

The crewmen had been at mess, and now those not on duty drifted aft to smoke and talk and reflect upon the dying day and what the morrow would bring. Probably not one of those present suspected he would never live to see it. When the search vessels and planes were called off several days later, the case was officially recorded as "unsolved." It became but another baffling incident in a series of strange marine disappearances, each leaving no trace, that have taken place in the past few years right at the back doorstep of the United States.

The region involved—a watery triangle bounded roughly by Florida, Bermuda, and Puerto Rico—measures less than a thousand miles on any one side. A small area on any mariner's map, it is hourly being ploughed by vessels of many nations. It is guarded over by radio. It is under constant surveillance from the dozens of commercial airliners that fly over it daily.

Yet its potential for mystery apparently remains just as great today as when Columbus first sailed its milk-green waters.

A Day That Will Live in Infamy

On Wednesday, December 5, 1945, five Navy *Avenger* type torpedo bombers roared away from the Naval Air Station at Fort Lauderdale, Florida. It was to have been a routine flight. It ended in one of the greatest peacetime searches in history. And, once more, not a single trace was found.

There were fourteen men aboard those bombers. As the hours passed anxious buddies back at the base and in other aircraft out on patrol listened hopefully to radio channels. But no word came to tell of the whereabouts of the missing flyers.

The last routine message, received at 5:25 that gusty afternoon, had given the position of the flight as seventy-five miles northeast of the Banana River (Florida) Naval Air Station, about 200 miles northeast of Miami.

The hands of the clock crawled around to the point where the bombers' fuel supply would be exhausted. Still no word. The Navy swung into action. Search planes and ships were ordered out to cover the entire area froin Key West northward to Jacksonville and 250 miles out to sea. For the benefit of the public the Navy pointed out tersely that the Avenger bomber was noted for its buoyancy. In similar emergencies such planes had always remained afloat long enough for the crews to launch the life rafts, often "without even getting their feet wet."

One of the first rescue craft to roar off in search of the missing fliers was a Navy PBM, a huge Martin Mariner bomber with a crew of thirteen that had been trained for just such work. This plane also disappeared without a trace. Interest in the disappearances now reached the stage where it dominated discussion in the streets. How could five bombers, each with its own crew and radio facilities, disappear from the face of the Earth without even flashing a single message of explanation? It was hardly logical to assume that the planes had collided in midair, killing all the crew members simultaneously. And, even were such a weird explanation acceptable, what about the PBM? What had happened to it?

A merchant ship, the S.S. *Gaines Mills*, sent a radio message to the Navy which described an explosion that had been observed high in the night sky at 7:50 P.M. that ill-fated Wednesday. The next morning, however, when planes and surface craft encircled the spot, no trace of wreckage or oil could be found. Already a huge search armada, headed up by the Navy escort carrier Solomons, had joined in the hunt. Hundreds of Army, Navy, and Coast Guard planes buzzed and banked over the sea. Seventeen assorted surface vessels churned the tropic waters. From the nearby territorial islands the British Royal Air Force pressed every available ship into service.

When the pilot of a commercial airline reported observing red flares and a campfire in the vicinity of Melbourne, Florida, the search was extended to land. Swamps were searched by marsh buggies, by jeep and on foot. All efforts proved in vain.

Commander Howard S. Robots, executive officer of the Fort Lauderdale base, said his airmen had apparently been blown off course by strong winds. The Miami Weather Bureau corroborated that freak winds, attended by gusts up to forty miles per hour, along with showers and occasional thunderstorms, had prevailed over the area of the last reported position. After this information the mystery enigma was to sink back into the depths of the sea. It would lie there, dormant, for three years. And then . . .

At 1:00 A.M. on Friday, January 30, 1948, disaster struck again. Once more it proved to be an aircraft, this time a heavy four-engined plane of the British South American Airways that bore the proud name *Star Tiger*. The ship was bound for Bermuda from the Azores. It had been overdue at Kindley Field, Bermuda, since 10:30 P.M. the night before. While still several hundred miles away from Kindley, the big *Tudor IV* airliner had sent its last message. There had been no indication of trouble, either with the aircraft or the twenty-three passengers and six crewmen aboard.

At dawn the search began. The U.S. Navy ordered ten surface vessels out. The weather was gloomy and fitful and got progressively worse. By late the following day strong seas were coursing through the desolate area, with gray-bearded waves forty feet high. It was no weather for flying. The thirty-odd Air Force Navy and civilian planes which had been fruitlessly searching the leaden waters were recalled. Once again mystery shrouded the victims, mystery that was deep, complete.

On March 5 of the same year, another disappearance took place, this one within a few miles of metropolitan Miami itself, in the shallow and relatively protected waters of Florida Bay. Here, for a change, some evidence of the grim ending would remain to mock the weary searchers.

Internationally famous horse racing jockey Al Snyder and two friends set out on a fishing expedition into the Florida Keys. Anchoring their cabin cruiser, the *Evelyn K.*, near Sandy Key, which lies about ten miles offshore Cape Sable, the southernmost part of the United States mainland, the three men set off in a small skiff to fish the surrounding shoals.

When they failed to return to the cruiser, the Coast Guard was notified. The usual search began. It started with several boats from nearby Everglades City, descending upon the site. These fishing skippers, sun-darkened men who had grown up in the Keys and who knew what it meant to be adrift beneath the burning sun, or worse, lost in the mosquito-ridden swamps without fresh water or anything better to eat than perhaps a few coon oysters, joined willingly with the Guardsmen in searching every likely spot.

By the end of the second day it became obvious that the search was accomplishing little. Then searchers found an oar identified as belonging to the missing skiff. Then a hat was found. By this time the army of searchers was increasing at an astounding rate. There were at least 800 people fine-combing the area, including Coast Guardsmen, sportsmen, fishing guides, and Army jungle combat teams in amphibious craft. One hundred boats of all descriptions churned the turquoise shoals of the bay. No less than fifty private and Armed Forces planes wheeled and dipped overhead, exploring every foot of the water and jungle patchwork below.

Then the skiff was found. Empty, it lay lodged in the mangrove roots of an unnamed island near Rabbit Key some sixty miles to the north of where the three men had set out.

The search was renewed with frantic vigor now. For the hours were growing short when missing men could remain alive without nourishment. Bloodhounds and guides led the way through the swamps and along the shorelines of silent lagoons. The missing jockey's wife refused to accept the inevitable. Friends of Snyder were inclined to agree with her. It just didn't make sense that with all the searchers and equipment at least one of the men, or his corpse, couldn't be recovered.

These same friends offered rewards totaling some $15,000 to anyone who could produce such conclusive evidence. A blimp was chartered—and inside it the worried turfmen flew over the atolls and headlands where Army helicopters still hovered and where foot soldiers thrashed through the underbrush, maintaining contact with walkie-talkies. But Al Snyder and his two companions were never seen again.

Trouble came again before the year was over. Captain Robert Linquist, of Fort Myers, Florida, sat at the controls of his DC-3 transport plane in the pre-dawn sky on December 28, 1948. The plane, operated by Airborne Transport, Inc., of New York City, had been chartered for a flight from San Juan, Puerto Rico, to Miami. Linquist's co-pilot was Ernie Hill, Jr., of Miami. Neither Floridian was a stranger to this particular run.The plane had safely covered all but five miles of the 1,000-mile trip. Lindquist had sent a radio message at 4:13 A.M. giving their position and explaining why they were slightly late (they had been due to land at Miami by 4:03 A.M.). Stewardess Mary

Burks may have stepped into the cabin about that time to serve the two pilots coffee and to comment on her thirty passengers, including two babies. The passengers, mostly Puerto Ricans, were returning to the States after spending the Christmas holiday on their native island.

It had been an easy trip, marked by good feeling all around. There had been some singing of Christmas carols and now all was quiet back in the darkened cabin. Although scattered clouds had ridden the night heavens with the DC-3, it had been smooth flying, with the slumbering little islands of the long Keys chain beginning to slip past far below (the U.S. Weather Bureau stated later there was no likelihood the plane had been forced down by bad weather). And then . . . disappearance. Abrupt. Complete. Not even a piece of torn, silver wreckage visible against the land when daylight came. Or an empty life jacket floating on the surface. Or even an unusually heavy concentration of sharks or barracuda in the clear water.

Again the search was launched from the air, from the water, and on the land. As many as forty-eight Coast Guard, Navy, and Air Force planes joined together in pinpointing the Florida Bay and Keys area, a region still fresh in memories from the Al Snyder incident. It was still the same shallow expanse of gin-clear water, only a fathom or two deep. A ship the size of the transport should be clearly visible even on the bottom.

The DC-3 had carried three ten-person life rafts and there had been life preservers for all the passengers. It even boasted a "Gibson Girl" portable radio transmitter for automatically sending SOS signals. No such signals were ever intercepted. A report that bodies had been sighted on a Cuban beach proved to be unfounded. But the search area was extended, nevertheless, to include the entire Caribbean and Gulf areas, as well as the southern tip of Florida in the Everglades region. By the third day squally weather sprang up to hamper the search. But it didn't matter, really. Nothing was ever found.

Sister Goes Missing

Three weeks later, a large task force of the U.S. Navy was on maneuvers south of Bermuda. The weather was good, the skies were clear, and the sea was calm. No one suspected that up there in those bright skies twenty people aboard a British South American Airways plane were hurrying to their deaths at 300 miles per hour. The Avro Tudor IV airliner known as the *Aerial* was a sister ship to the other four-engined craft that had been lost in the area less than a year before. With thirteen passengers and crew of six Captain J. G. McPhee took off from Bermuda at 7:42 A.M., Monday, January 17, 1949. He was en route to Kingston, Jamaica, five hours and fifteen minutes away to the south. The 1,000-mile hop was to have taken them farther along on their regularly scheduled trip which had begun in London and would end when they reached Santiago, Chile.

For the five-hour trip, the plane carried ten hours' worth of fuel. When they were 180 miles south of Bermuda (about an hour after departure) Captain McPhee, a veteran ocean flier, sent a radio message advising that he was changing frequencies to pick up Kingston's ground control. That was the last ever heard from the *Aerial*. No SOS. No hint of trouble. Nothing. Soon the radio wavelengths were crackling with terse messages between Bermuda, Kingston, and Miami. The Coast Guard air-sea rescue headquarters at Miami ordered out rescue planes from as far away as Massachusetts. The Fifth Rescue Squadron of the Air Force, stationed a MacDill Field, Tampa, likewise became airborne. Word was flashed to the Navy task force already in the vicinity. Two 27,000-ton carriers immediately joined in the search. Other units were diverted. The U.S.S. *Kearsarge* and *Leyte* headed up one group of ships to the north side of the island of Cuba. Included in this group were the light cruisers *Fargo*, *Portsmouth*, and *Huntington*, aided by six destroyers.

Searching to the south of the island, between Cuba and Kingston, the 45,000-ton *Missouri* led a pack consisting of the light cruiser *Juneau* and four destroyer mine-sweepers. The disappearance jinx would be broken now or never. Probably never again would there be an opportunity like this. Six of the Coast Guard's two-engined PBM patrol planes now augmented dozens of craft put aloft by the *Kearsarge* and the *Leyte*. Two merchant ships likewise turned from their courses to aid in the hunt. Thousands of sharp eyes, trained for just such work, scanned the surface of the smiling sea. All in vain.

There have been other disappearances in this backyard sea of ours: the Government and private aircraft, fishing boats, yachts. And always the record, when the account is finally closed, has the ominous notation: "No trace found."

Atlantis: Land Under the Sea

Ignatius Donnelly: Visionary of Atlantis

Frank Joseph

August 1989

Donnelly, more than anyone, recognized modern America's parallel with old Atlantis

Alone and surrounded only by the high shelves of his beloved books, the short, stocky man sat writing at a walnut desk. In the middle of the room, a Franklin stove shed radiance and warmth throughout the library, while the blunt-edged winds of a Minnesota autumn battered the window panes. He wrote by the steady, yellow beam of an oil lamp, but his thoughts were as bleak as the darkness outside gathering against the midnight.

Today was his birthday, made all the more poignant, sad and ironic by the loving congratulations bestowed on him earlier in the day by his adoring family. Undistracted now, he vented all his heartache into the pages of his diary.

> November 3, 1880. Alas and alack! Today is my forty-ninth birthday, and a sad day it is. All my hopes are gone, and the future settles down upon me dark and gloomy indeed. My life has been a failure and a mistake. My hopes have so often come to naught that I cease to hope. Well, well. All I can do is to face the music and take my damnable fortune as it comes. A gloomy view for a man entering on his fiftieth year!

He closed the little notebook and stared into the lamplight. His mind raced over the years that had brought him to this point. The utopian dream of building an ideal community on the banks of the Mississippi had gone bankrupt. Once lieutenant governor of the state, his political career lay in ruins. All his hard labor as publisher and editor had come to nothing. Even a farming enterprise in nearby Stevens County, hit by drought and locusts, was collapsing. Bedeviled by mounting debts and mortified by his inability to better provide for the family, he pushed away from the desk and strode across the room in an effort to shake off his care. He ran the strong fingers of his small hands through his thick, auburn hair, took a deep breath, then let it out in a sigh of resignation.

Turning for consolation to his cherished volumes neatly stacked against all four walls, his eye fell on a lidless, half-forgotten box hiding in a dark corner of the library. He knew what it contained and carried it back to his desk and into the light. He vaguely skimmed over the huge collection of written material, the result of many years of personal research in his hometown,

Philadelphia, and in the Library of Congress at Washington, D.C. All his life, he had been an avid history buff, and his voracious reading tended toward understanding the saga of human history from ancient times. But for all his study he could not discover what he felt must have been a missing link between the savage and the civilized man, a lost piece in the puzzle of human origins. The mystery assumed an importance in his mind on a par with the political problems of his own day. All the time he played at founding father, gentleman farmer, publisher and politician, the question preoccupied him, simmering on the back burners of his high-powered imagination: Where and how did civilization first arise? The answer, he believed, lay somewhere in all those thousands of notes.

In a lightning flash of recognition, the night's despair vanished at once. A new plan, a fresh hope, sprang full-blown in his mind. He would organize the haphazard material into a book unprecedented and controversial in approach, yet buttressed by impressive documentary sources and logical argument; its publication must ensure success. With it he would win the glory and income denied him by all previous endeavors. Past failures and present disappointments melted away in a blaze of intense creativity. The man's brain was afire with purpose, ideas and expression. By mid-March the following year the work was done, and he entrained to New York with his loosely bound manuscript in search of a publishing contract

The trip from St. Paul took four hours and cost him $30.00, first class. Once in New York City, he started at the top with the country's biggest publisher, Harper's, and struck pay dirt. The editors were so taken with his research that they not only agreed to publish it but, just as importantly, planned to actively promote it. On his return to Minnesota, the new author stopped over at Chicago's famous Palmer House to treat himself to a lavish steak dinner for thirty-five cents. On July 22, he received the first galley sheets from Harper's and exclaimed in his diary, "I feel like a mother listening to the first cry of her first born. It may grow up to be an imbecile, but the fibers of my heart will cling to it."

Receiving extensive, almost universally favorable reviews in the country's leading newspapers, response to the book out-stripped his highest hopes. Seven years after its release it had gone through twenty-three American editions, with an additional twenty-six British editions, leaping overnight from a national to an international best-seller. When a four-page personal letter arrived from the famous British Prime Minister, William Gladstone, congratulating him on his effort, the Minnesota writer confided to his diary, "I looked down at myself and could not but smile at the appearance of the man who, in this little snowbound hamlet, was corresponding with the man whose word was fate anywhere in the British Empire. The leg of my pants was torn; my coat was nearly buttonless." But in a short time, the success Ignatius Donnelly received from *Atlantis, the Antediluvian World* put buttons on his coat—gold ones. He had come a long way since that night of despair on his forty-nineth birthday.

His was a strange, fateful book by a strange and driven man. With its publication, Ignatius Donnelly became the founder of modern Atlantology, the study of Atlantean civilization. Until his research, Atlantis was little more than a collective-conscious dream in the imagination of poets. Although alluded to in the prehistoric traditions of many cultures around the world, the earliest known account of Atlantis was composed during the early fourth century B.C., in two Dialogues, the *Timaeus* and the *Critias*, by the Greek philosopher Plato. According to Plato, the original report was brought to Greece 200 years earlier by Solon, the famous Athenian lawgiver, who heard it recounted firsthand by the chief Priest in the Temple of the Goddess Neith (roughly, the Egyptian counterpart of Athena) at Sais. No literary invention, the tablets inscribed with the account were to be seen for centuries after Plato's death. One of his followers, Krantor, an illustrious philosopher in his own right, personally traveled in 260 B.C. to Lower Egypt, where he found Plato's narrative enshrined detail for detail.

Krantor was also a respected scholar at the great library of Alexandria, the Ancient World's center of classical learning. There the story of Atlantis was regarded as a credible episode in early history by the leading minds of the age, including Strabo, chief chronicler of the Roman Empire.

Referring to the research of a Spanish historian (Poseidonous of Rhodes), he wrote, "He did well in citing the opinion of Plato that the tradition concerning the island of Atlantis might be received as something more than fiction."

Briefly, Plato's story tells of a great city that flourished in pre-classical times on an Atlantic island outside the Straits of Gibraltar. Atlantis was the capital of a materially prosperous and politically powerful empire with all the scientific technology and artistic splendor of a high civilization. Although its people were traditionally virtuous and wise, successive generations gradually yielded to avarice and aggression, finally engaging in an imperialist war against Greece and Egypt. During this period of far-flung hostilities, Atlantis was suddenly wracked by massive geologic violence which, "in a single day and night," carried the entire island and most of its inhabitants to the bottom of the sea.

The great library contained a wealth of material describing Atlantis. Virtually all of it was lost when the magnificent building was torched by religious fanatics at the close of the Roman Empire. Plato's story was condemned as heresy by churchmen on two counts: Atlantis did not appear in the Bible and it did not fit into the curious chronology of theologians who dated God's creation of the world to 5508 B.C.

During the ensuing Dark Ages ushered in by the collapse of the classical world, Atlantis, along with most of the achievements of ancient civilization, was forgotten. A thousand years later, as the Renaissance got under way, Plato's story was resurrected by Spanish explorers who were struck by obvious comparisons between the New World they were conquering and the "Outer Continent" described in the Atlantis account. Athanasius Kircher, the German genius of the seventeenth century; Francisco Lopez Gomara, Madrid's royal cartographer; and Sir Francis Bacon, who was, almost 300 years later, to play a major role in the life of Ignatius Donnelly, were among the intellectual luminaries who revived serious interest in the lost island-capital.

But they were unable to add anything new to Plato's report. Over the next three centuries, Atlantis was slipping back into the realm of fable and could more often be found as a recurring theme in Western literature, most famously in Jules Verne's novel *20,000 Leagues Under the Sea*, and Edgar Allan Poe's verse *The City in the Sea*. Donnelly's great achievement was to apply the scientific method to Plato's story thereby elevating it from a questionable historical narrative into a credible document. He bolstered his modern approach with the latest findings in geology, botany, comparative mythology, archaeology, anthropology, and linguistics, and presented his argument in a clear, rational, persuasive, highly readable exposition. His conclusions took him far beyond the Greek account to show that Atlantis was the very fountainhead of earthly civilization, the place where humanity first rose from barbarism to organized society, and the original source from which the earliest high cultures on both sides of the Atlantic Ocean derived. It was a startling, entirely novel deduction, but the logical marshalling of abundant, up-to-date source material seemed irrefutable.

The popularity he experienced as the founder of Atlantology surpassed his reputation as a statesman because even old political enemies, such as those at the *St. Paul Dispatch*, could not help but publicly admire his effort as the author of one of the notable books of the century. His Atlantis was the theme of both the New Orleans' Mardi Gras and the Baltimore Oriole Festival in 1883. Three years later, he was good-naturedly declared the "Duke of Atlantis" in St. Paul's Winter Carnival. As his biographer wrote, "Thousands of people who normally did not read or hear of current books were exposed to Donnelly's work and many of them bought it."

But why did this book, as interesting as it was, generate such a widespread enthusiasm among the common people, as well as the intelligentsia of the world? An explanation may be found in the times themselves, and especially in a general mood that prevailed largely unspoken among late nineteenth century Americans. They felt that with the disastrous Civil War and the rise of industrial high finance in its aftermath, the country had entered into a serious departure from the spiritual or idealistic path it began in the previous century. America, they knew, was born with the glorious expedition of Columbus, got a foothold through the selfless rigors of the pilgrims, grew into the greatest political achievement in history and expanded across a vast continent of unlimited wealth and beauty. This grand epic of liberty was achieved through individual heroism, self-reliance, rugged idealism, and a feeling of community with other Americans. These seemed to be peculiarly American virtues that were being steadily debased into mere shop talk for ambitious politicians.

Atlantis, too, had been a great, happy nation—powerful, expansive, rich, a beacon of freedom and enlightenment for the rest of the world. But a war interrupted the peaceful course of her civilization. Her people turned away from the ethical standards and idealism of their ancestors in the selfish pursuit of materialism. They allowed themselves to fall from being a noble race honoring liberty and nature to a debased rabble interested only in shallow self-gratification and the endless pursuit of wealth. For this betrayal of their former greatness, the gods sent Atlantis a catastrophe so horrific that memory of it was seared forever into the collective consciousness of humanity and vented in the so-called flood legends of the world. Perhaps, many intuited, heaven was preparing a similar fate for an America that was learning how to compromise its old principles with new greeds.

The ominous parallel between pre-deluge Atlantis and nineteenth-century America did not go unnoticed and that awareness accounted for its underlying fascination. The appearance of Donnelly's book could not have been more timely. Atlantis was and is a history lesson that should be learned; therein lies its significance. It is not to know that Atlantis was the origin of civilization, and that its people were highly gifted in the arts and sciences while Egypt and Sumer were still vacant deserts. "We cannot escape history." The portentous words of President Lincoln still rang in the thoughts of Americans who saw in Donnelly's lost island an unsettling reflection of their own society.

Ignatius Donnelly was the perfect, indeed, the only man who could have brought Atlantis back to life. The job was too big for a trained scientist, especially a Victorian Age scientist who was really a narrow specialist indoctrinated in the restricted discipline of the time. Donnelly possessed two virtues that qualified him for his task. He had, by all accounts, a truly encyclopedic mind that ranged authoritatively over an enormous variety of subjects. An insatiable, rapid reader since youth, his persistent curiosity and passionate interest in life made him a renaissance man on a grand scale. It was not for nothing that he was known as the Sage of Nininger, the town he helped to found in the 1850s.

Just as importantly, Donnelly had a fervent devotion to the truth. Yet, he bewildered his contemporaries because he changed his political affiliations with as much facility as other men changed their coats. His alliances, quickly assumed and cast off in turn—from Republican to Democrat to all kinds of independent affiliations—ranked him a hypocrite and a crass opportunist in the eyes of many. To them he seemed "a veritable conundrum with the key thrown away," "a cryptogram and its key lost." Even long after his death, "his inconsistencies and consistencies alike baffle understanding." But his mercurial political allegiances were only expedients. However inflexible he may have been in his ideals, he was very flexible in the means he employed to effect their realization. As the modern historian of Nininger rightly puts it, "It was the political parties that were inconsistent, and Donnelly merely aligned himself with the party that most favorably promoted his point of view. He was a man concerned with the wisdom and principles of government, rather than politics for the purpose of personal or partisan gains."

It was, however, just this freedom of intellect that made it possible for him to collect the vast material evidence for Atlantis and present it in a clearly understandable fashion. And in this he revealed himself not as an intellectual snob seeking to impress his learned colleagues with his great brain, but as a true scholar, who strove to make an important message accessible to all. As one recent commentator wrote rightfully of

Donnelly, "Unquestionably, there was something in his message and his personality, insofar as it shaped that message, which a significant body of his contemporaries found appealling."

And Donnelly, more than anyone, recognized modern America's parallel with old Atlantis. He knew from personal experience what it was like to battle as a state senator and congressman against a soulless money-power on behalf of farmers and miners. It was a fight he was to lose, but he learned a broader lesson from defeat and transformed personal failure into the disturbing historical irony implicit in his *Antediluvian World.*

Even before its first edition had gone to press, Donnelly was already hot at work on a sequel. Recurring throughout his voluminous collection of mythic traditions from around the world was an explicit theme describing a cataclysmic celestial occurrence he interpreted as a comet's collision with the Earth. He felt the event tended to reveal something about the nature of the destruction of Atlantis, but in 1882 there was not enough supportive data available for him to establish a connection. Based on the geological findings of his day, he concluded that the last Ice Age was caused by a comet strike. Although wrong, he was less wrong than his scientifically-trained contemporaries who believed ice ages resulted from shifts in the Earth's axis or reversals of its magnetic field. Only as late as the 1970s have geophysicists and astronomers generally concurred that our planet's ice ages seem intimately associated with sunspot activity.

While the chief argument in *Ragnarok* (named after the Norse legend of a cosmic disaster, *Twilight of the Gods*) has been faulted by scientific discoveries made nearly one hundred years later, the book's secondary theme is not only persistently valid but extremely visionary. Donnelly was the first writer to assert that the Earth has been visited many times throughout its history by extraterrestrial catastrophes. It was this point, more than his theory of the Ice Ages, that was lampooned and almost universally rejected in his own day and far into the next century. Only a few fringe theorists (Bellamy, Hoerbiger and Vilikovsky), disdained by establishment academics as "crackpots," followed up on Donnelly's discovery, which he deduced largely through his brilliant examination of the consistency of mythic traditions in the Old and New Worlds.

It was not until the 1930s that Arizona's Meteor Crater was officially recognized by scientists as the result of a major impact. Forty years later, the sudden extinction of the dinosaurs was linked to an asteroid collision with the Earth, a theory that has gained credence as new and supportive evidence has come to light. In the 1980s some astronomers concluded that our Moon was formed after a massive object, perhaps a planetoid, smashed into the young Earth, gouging out colossal quantities of debris and hurling them into space, where they were caught in the Earth's gravitational field and, over the eons, coalesced into our one and only natural satellite. With the advent of aerial photography, especially orbital photography, literally hundreds of impact craters, some as big as forty miles across, have been verified on the face of the globe.

Donnelly's hunch that an extraterrestrial event was somehow responsible for the Atlantis catastrophe was given great assistance by one of Germany's pioneer space scientists, a colleague of Dr. Werner von Braun employed as a research expert at the famous rocket testing center, Peenemunde. Inventor of the snorkel, a major technological advance in the development of the modern submarine, Otto Muck demonstrated that two deep-sea holes off the South Carolina coast were major impact craters formed by a disintegrating asteroid that struck the ocean bottom and set off a chain reaction of seismic violence along the Mid-Atlantic Ridge, a geologically unstable gash in the seafloor on which Plato's island stood. Muck's unimpeachable scientific credentials, together with the factual argument brought to bear in his book, *The Secret of Atlantis*, have not been faulted since its publication in 1965.

Donnelly began work on *God and the Sun*, an examination of Atlantean religion, only three days after completing *Ragnarok*. But the violent rejection of *Ragnarok*, so far ahead of its time, discouraged him and he returned to politics, leaving the manuscript sadly incomplete.

Today, opponents of arguemnts on behalf of Atlantis enjoy ripping his work from the comfortable vantage point of the late twentieth century, faulting his geology and ridiculing his interpretations of the evidence. But even that unsympathetic critic, E. F. Bleiler, writes, "Surprisingly enough, Donnelly was pretty much abreast of the American archaeology of his day. In Middle and South America, too, Donnelly was reasonably up to date. Much the same holds true for Donnelly's Old World archaeology. As far as anthropology proper goes, here, Donnelly knew and utilized important language books."

It is, after all, his interpretation of comparative myth that has most successfully withstood the passage of time. Some of his geology has not fared well, but that should hardly be surprising in view of the huge strides made in the earth sciences over the last century. Donnelly employed state-of-the-art geology, and it is both ignorant and unfair to belittle the level of knowledge achieved by our predecessors. It is a remarkable tribute to Ignatius Donnelly that so much of his work has not only been verified by subsequent research, but at least some of his insights have proved absolutely visionary.

Nor is it meant here to suggest that his geology is entirely worthless. Some of his deductions in this field are no less ahead of their time than his explorations of Atlantean mythic traditions within New World cosmogonies. While Atlantis was not, as he concluded, a true continent with physical land bridges connecting South America, his analysis of the Mid-Atlantic Ridge anticipated by eighty years the deep-water discoveries achieved by sonar: "Along a great line, a mighty fracture in the surface of the globe, stretching north and south through the Atlantic, we find a continuous series of active or extinct volcanoes." Seafloor lava flows were not photographically documented until the 1970s, yet Donnelly wrote in 1881 that "the great fires which destroyed Atlantis are still smoldering in the depths of the ocean."

Establishment academics do not hate Donnelly because some of his research is dated or his conclusions wrong. If that were the case, they would have ample cause to despise Kepler, Newton, Darwin and every research genius in history. Donnelly is officially condemned because he did not belong to the professional club of college pass-men and the holders of degrees. Worse, he succeeded in popularizing science and history without the benefit of university training, but entirely through the power of his original and imaginative intellect.

Previous to its release, Donnelly worried in his diary that *The Antediluvian World* would be a failure "because I am a provincial in location and a nobody in the scientific world; for mankind always looks to Jerusalem and thinks it impossible that any good thing can come out of Nazareth. It is difficult for a new man to get anyone to believe in him." But in the first chapter of his own book, he showed greater self-assurance: "The fact that the history of Atlantis was for thousands of years regarded as a fable proves nothing. There is an unbelief which grows out of ignorance, as well as a skepticism which is born of intelligence. The people nearest the past are not always those who are best informed concerning the past." This early statement wonderfully sets the even-handed tone for the whole argument that follows.

A better appreciation of Donnelly is possible when the deplorable conditions of nineteenth-century American academics is understood. Science and history were stultifying in an elitism that was putting distance between the country's intelligentsia and its common people. In one stroke, *The Antediluvian World* bridged that widening abyss and awakened the imagination of millions to the consideration of life's higher, nobler questions. The popular awakening generated by his book must have been particularly gratifying for a man who always believed his greatest achievement was the creation of the National Bureau of Education, passed by the House in 1866, the birth of public education in America.

Since its first publication more than one hundred years ago, four generations of readers have experienced *The Antediluvian World* as a mind-expanding adventure. It is still enormously readable. The writing breezes along with an earnest exuberance as the author unfolds all the fascinating details collected over so many years of research. Its excitement is contagious, and the book leaves most readers thoughtful at least. Lewis Spence, the great Scottish mythographer who followed Donnelly as the leading Atlantologist in the first half of the twentieth century, admitted that "any departure from his general method would be as vain as it would be unintelligent. The blueprints were there and their impressive outlines must be followed." Spence affirmed that this method, "in its correctness and integrity, remains unchallenged."

More than 5,000 books and leading articles about Atlantis in some twenty languages over the last 100 years are directly descended from *The Antediluvian World*, which is still the best of its kind. What strikes the reader of this book, besides the awe and enthusiasm obviously felt by the author, is Donnelly's rescue of the Atlantis question from the lifeless discussion of a dead past. He carried it into the contemporary spotlight and beyond, into future prospects, a visionary quality that permeates the whole work; one reason for its perennial relevance and evident from the opening chapter: "Further investigations and discoveries will, I trust, confirm the correctness of the conclusions at which I have arrived."

In both *The Antediluvian World* and *Ragnarok*, Atlantean research, newly born, had gone just about as far as it could within the technological limitations of the nineteenth century. Scientific archaeology was itself not much older. Although he continued to lecture widely about Atlantis, Donnelly was drawn back into the political arena with all its duplicity and disappointment. As he wrote later, "One thing is certain—my books have lifted me out of the dirty cesspool of politics, nasty enough at all times, but absolutely foul to the man who does not win."

Donnelly was not mired in contemplation of the preshistoric past, for all his years of intense study. His mind operated freely over time with wonderful facility because he disregarded rigid conventional divisions of past, present and future. History, modern life and what was to come were all woven of the same cloth, to his way of thinking.

Donnelly's political activities were subsequently far ahead of his time, which accounts for their lack of success. Many of his reformist views are amazingly in line with some of the hottest issues in the 1980s. He was the first American statesman to work for protection of the environment. On July 15, 1868, he urged, for the first time in Congressional history, the planting of forests on public lands by the federal government. He advocated universal public education for all people, and he was an outspoken champion of women's suffrage. In a typically

Donnelly-style comparison, he declared, "Woman, it is urged, is physically weaker than man. That proves nothing. The right to vote is not a question of physical strength. If it were, the pugilist would have more votes than the philosopher."

Ignatius Donnelly died of a heart attack in St. Paul, as the hour struck midnight on January 1, 1901. The singular propriety of that moment implies an otherworldly significance precisely poised between two centuries. For a man who bestrode time with such deftness and agility, the instant of his death could not have been more appropriate or better timed to characterize a life of historical consciousness and futuristic vision—a perfectly dramatic exit for a dramatic actor.

Like many idealists unable to realize their highest hopes, Ignatius Donnelly considered himself a failure, an opinion seconded by his contempoary and future detractors. Indeed, his attempts to found a successful utopian community and his life-long struggle for national reform came to nothing. But almost ninety years after his death his name and thoughts are rising again. His spirit seems as irrepressible as ever. His most enduring book, *Atlantis, the Antediluvian World*, is still in print throughout our world.

Atlantis Rising in the Bahamas?

Neil Slocum
April 1994

Ancient ruins hint to a civilization that once inhabited this island paradise.

At a depth of about twenty feet, in the warm, clear waters of the Atlantic, a short boat ride from Bimini island in the Bahamas, scuba divers can drift slowly over the Bimini Road. Sometimes called the Atlantean Wall, the feature appears to be a series of large blocks, carefully placed there by some intelligence.

Within a radius of a few miles of the site, are foundations of large and small buildings, geometric designs, and what appear to be the remains of a seaport. All of these mysterious structures are under water in areas that have not been dry land for 10,000 years, at least since the last ice age.

Almost no archaeological work has been done here. Few, if any, orthodox archaeologists are willing to spend any time on what seems to them to be an anomaly of little significance.

Many of these artifacts were discovered by Dr. Hanson Valentine, Dimitri Rebikoff, and Robert Marx in the late 1960s. They believed the structures were pre-Columbian in origin and that they could not have been constructed by the local Lucayan Indians in residence at the time of Columbus.

In 1975 and 1977, Dr. David Zink, a scuba diver, a sailor, and a student of ancient civilizations, led expeditions to study the construction. He concluded that the Bimini Road was neither a road nor a wall, but a structure that was used for astronomy. He also came to believe that the stones were enormously old.

If any of these theories about the Bimini wall are proven true, they could have a dramatic and startling effect on modern scholarship. The least significant revelation the undersea construction might hold could be evidence of Phoenician or early European contact with the New World. At best, the massive blocks and structures could at last be positive evidence of lost Atlantis. The real puzzle is why no one wants to study this relatively easily accessible area.

Perhaps the reason lies in archaeology itself. Far from being the dry study of ancient tools, archaeology today is filled with controversy, conflict, and political correctness.

Archaeologists pride themselves on being coldly scientific, yet, in spite of strong evidence, many refuse to accept that a large number of great archaeological discoveries were either made by gifted amateurs or made possible by amateur interest.

Schliemann's discovery of ancient Troy is the most outstanding case in point. There are others: Carter's discovery of the tomb of Tutankhamen would not have been possible without the study, interest, and support of Lord Carnarvon. The discovery of *The Monitor*, the Civil War vessel, was made by a dedicated scuba diver, and amateur Hiram Bingham's discovery of Machu Picchu added luster to the discoveries of non-professionals.

In the world of undersea archaeology, there is practically no wreck, sunken temple, or inundated city ruin that has not been discovered by amateurs. Although amateur theories are sometimes wrong, the enthusiasm and drive brought to the search for treasure has advanced human knowledge of the past. In general, the members of the academically trained archaeological community are rarely discoverers and explorers. They seem inordinately willing to attack the theories of amateurs, while simultaneously advancing their own careers based on amateurs' discoveries.

A Sea Lane

The Bahamas lie in a strategic location that has been a sea lane since earliest known times. Because of winds and currents, many of the great Spanish treasure flotas (or fleets) passed by the islands. Many of these were wrecked, as were other ships and boats through the ages. Scuba divers know that a visit to Bimini can be an incredible experience filled with new and exotic sights.

With the great explosion in the popularity of scuba diving since the 1970s, formerly remote islands, atolls, and shoals have become accessible to ever greater numbers of divers. Some of these people are surprised to find experiences they didn't count on when they began their dive.

Although debunkers insist that the Bimini road is natural, a diver who observes the feature through the dappled sunlight of the warm tropical sea knows without doubt that he or she is looking at a humanly constructed object. The huge stones are evenly placed in a J-shaped pattern that does not occur naturally. Some divers have reported finding classical, fluted columns and fitted stones made of a marble that is not found locally. There is some sea growth and crystallization on and between the stones, and the feeling of being in the presence of something extremely old is very powerful to a sensitive diver.

Not all the structures under water in this region are found so easily, but many of them can be seen from the air and later located by boats with modern, sophisticated bottom locators. Divers must generally charter their own boats to seek out the ruins, since the commercial boats visit other dive spots.

Cayce Prediction Fulfilled?

The famous psychic Edgar Cayce predicted that "Atlantis will rise near Bimini" in 1968 or 1969. This prediction seems to be coming true, albeit belatedly, as the sea floor is apparently slowly rising. More and more geometric-shaped structures are emerging from their sand coverings each year, and determined divers can find them with a little energy and scientific searching.

One story circulating around Bimini is that the structures were built by early twentieth-century sponge divers to hold their sponges while they looked for more. Supposedly, there is a ninety-year-old former sponger who remembers building one of them. Unfortunately, no one seems to know the former diver and he has never been located.

The major structures simply could not have been made by divers who did not have the benefit of oxygen tanks. The stones are massive and firmly placed in a deliberate design and pattern. They were either made with heavy equipment or built on land with the aid of unlimited manpower.

Although additional exploration work was done in the 1970s and 1980s, it was mainly of a surveying nature. Real underwater excavation of the type done regularly in the Mediterranean has yet to be undertaken, and the artifacts of civilization—tools, utensils, and pottery shards—still have not been found.

Before making quick judgments or formulating wild theories, more study needs to be done. That the structures were planned and carried out for a purpose can hardly be doubted, but what the purpose might be can hardly be imagined.

Were these structures Phoenician, Egyptian, Mayan, or even antediluvian Atlantean? This question and all the others related to it need to be answered. Earth's history in terms of geological time is incredibly long, and humans have been the dominant species for only a second of this immense time period. But perhaps these undersea finds will force us to revise our estimates of how long modern humans have been on the scene.

Did beings from other planets colonize and flourish during the unimaginably long time that Earth has existed? In the cycles of geological renewal over millions of years, are there still some signs of civilizations so remote that we can't conceive of them? Perhaps the Bimini Road, the building foundations, the designs, and the seaport are not from Atlantis, but perhaps they are. It's time to do some serious work and solve the mystery.

Atlantis: History's Most Enduring Riddle

Margaret Lougee Bowers
June 1971

So far the evidence warrants a healthy skepticism—but our generation may find the answers.

Atlantis—the fabled lost continent which has been called the cradle of humankind, the navel of the ocean, the island of the cities of gold—still awaits discovery. As our knowledge of the distant past continues to grow we find the age of civilized humans is far greater than we suspected. And there still is a great deal to be learned. Beneath the Earth lies history untouched by the archaeologist's spade. Beneath the sea even more surprising antiquities one day may be discovered—or, given the nature of the Earth's ever-changing, shifting crust, may rise again in all their forgotten splendor.

The world's greatest mystery story began more than 2,400 years ago in ancient Greece when Plato penned the first account of a highly developed people who dwelt on a series of islands beyond the Gates of Hercules. In two dialogues, the *Timeus* and the *Critias*, he describes how the main island, Atlantis (or Poseidon), and the others together formed a "mighty power which was aggressing wantonly against the whole of Europe and Asia." This empire "had rule over the whole island and several others, as well as over parts of the continent; and, besides these, they subjected the parts of Libya as far as Egypt, and of Europe as far as Tyrrhenia."

The "continent" he refers to well may be America for he explains that Atlantis was so close to the Pillars of Hercules (the straits of Gibraltar) that only a harbor separated them. The traveler might pass through these islands to the "real sea" and from there to the "surrounding land" which "may be most truly called a continent." Plato seems to have had his geography straight enough.

Those who dismiss Plato's narrative as mere fabrication often fail to take note of other historians of antiquity who mention Atlantis as a matter of factual record—some, like Diodorus (in the third book of his *World History*), independently of Plato. Aristotle, who disbelieved in Atlantis, nonetheless wrote of a large island in the Atlantic which the Carthaginians called Antillia. Krantor (fourth century B.C.) reported that he had seen the Egyptian columns on which the written story of Atlantis was preserved. Strabo and Pomponius Mela (first century Romans) confirm its historical existence as does Theopompus of Chios (fourth century Greek). Plutarch refers to islands and a continent in the Atlantic. One of them, Ogygia, also appears in *The Odyssey* in the eighth century B.C. *The Odyssey*, we should remember, was merely the first written record of historical adventures passed down by word of mouth for centuries before Homer's time.

Marcelinus and Proclus, third and fourth Century Romans respectively, confirm that Atlantis was sacred to Poseidon and tell of its eventual destruction. Herodotus (fifth century Greek) claims that "the first of the Greeks to perform long voyages" knew of a city called Tartessos "beyond the Pillars of Hercules" where these early traders "made by the return voyage a profit more than any Greeks before their day." Tertullian, Philo Judaeus, and Arnobius Afer all comment on a tremendous upheaval in the Atlantic that swallowed up huge islands and the land bridge that once joined Sicily to Italy disappeared beneath the sea, leaving the Sicilian Strait in its wake.

An especially intriguing record, now lost, supposedly told of an Egyptian expedition sent by a pharaoh of the Second Dynasty to learn whether anything remained of Atlantis. According to the record, the expedition returned after five years with only negative answers.

Plato's legacy provides a description of the Atlanteans, their geography, their architecture, their rulers and social order, even their dress and customs. He claims that in the beginning the gods divided the Earth among themselves. "Poseidon, receiving for his lot the island of Atlantis, begat children by a mortal woman and settled them in a part of the island." He tells how the mighty empire began to degenerate from within until at length "there occurred violent earthquakes and floods, and in a single day and night all your warlike men in a body sank into the Earth, and the island of

Atlantis in like manner disappeared beneath the sea." Plato remarks it was the decision of the "god of gods" to punish them for the wretched state into which they had fallen.

If the foregoing sounds familiar, refer to Genesis 6:2-7: "The sons of God saw the daughters of men that they were fair; and they took them wives all of which they chose . . . and they bare children to them, the same became mighty men which were of old, men of renown. And God saw that the wickedness of man was great in the Earth . . . and the Lord said, I will destroy man whom I have created from the face of the Earth."

His method, of course, was what Biblical writers believed to be a universal flood. It is not unlikely that both accounts, which parallel each other so closely, have their roots in the same primeval cataclysm. In both cases destruction was by water and the land destroyed was the cradle of civilization. Initially men lived there in bliss but became corrupt through intermarriage with an inferior race and the Creator elected to punish them by "total" destruction. Could the "mighty men of old" in Genesis have been the Atlanteans themselves—of whom Noah was one of the survivors?

All countries from Great Britain to North Africa, through the Canaries and the Azores and on to the Americas—all of these bordering the Atlantic—cherish lgends that seem to refer to this great land. Peoples of the eastern Atlantic coast point to the west for their primordial origins while those of the west coast claim their ancestors arrived from the east. The mythologies of the Chaldeans, the Hindus, the Moslems, the Greeks, the Welsh, the Scandinavians and the Indians of North, Central, and South America all contain deluge legends—some with rather curious angles—that parallel the Hebraic flood.

The hero of the Aztec story, for example, is named Nata (Noah). The Toltecs trace their origin back to a country named Atlan, which the Aztecs called Aztlan. The records of numerous North American tribes claim their ancestors migrated from an eastern land which was destroyed in a deluge and many preserve the image of the ark or the dove in their myths. The legends of the Hopis are remarkably similar to those of the Biblical Hebrews. So are the ancient rituals they practice to this day.

Heinrich Schliemann in the last century and Thor Heyerdahl in our own have found that legend, however archaic, has its origin in fact. Significantly the flood legends appear only among peoples living on landmasses within reach of men who might have abandoned a sinking island in the mid-Atlantic. Indeed the Atlanteans may have established colonies in many of these areas before the deluge.

But what about Egypt? Its strategic location would lead one to expect that it too would preserve a flood legend. Since it does not, we must return to Plato for the answer.

Plato relates that his ancestor Solon, while visiting in Egypt, met with the priests of Sais, who were well versed in matters of antiquity. When Solon attempts to reckon the dates of certain events, one of the older priests tells him that he is a mere child in matters of ancient science and tradition.

"What do you mean?" Solon asks. The priest proceeds to discuss certain episodes in the distant past and reflects on the nature of world history—suggesting the existence of a tremendously old and methodically written historical record. The Egyptians had no flood "legend" because their history recorded the destruction of Atlantis and they knew there had been no "universal" flood.

"There have been and there will be again," says the priest, "many destructions of mankind arising out of many causes . . . . You remember one deluge only, whereas there were many before that." He adds that by virtue of their location in the Nile Valley the Egyptians have escaped both floods and conflagrations and consequently "the things preserved here are said to be the oldest." In fact he maintains that the Egyptians have preserved in their temples records of all important events known to have occurred in the lands they were familiar with.

In modern times the great American psychic Edgar Cayce gave numerous readings on the subject of Atlantis. He claimed that the history of Atlantis as a continent began about 25,000 B.C. About 12,000 B.C. earthquakes and volcanic action caused the landmass to begin to break up into islands.

From 12,000 to 10,000 B.C. many of its citizens migrated to established colonies in Spain, France, Egypt, Central America, and what is now the southwestern United States, where they introduced arts, letters, medicine, monotheism and other accouterments of a highly developed culture.

According to the testimony of geology and oceanography there is little doubt that a landmass, or series of islands, once existed in the Atlantic. To begin with, the entire stretch of the north and mid-Atlantic is geologically unstable and prone to seismic and volcanic disturbances. Even today, as the landmasses of the southern hemisphere rise, the coastline of Greenland is sinking so rapidly that inhabitants no longer build anywhere near the shoreline. The shallow limestone banks off the Bahamas, which drop suddenly into the abysmal Tongue of the Ocean, and are riddled with deep sinkholes, some boring to depths of 200 feet and more; these sinkholes were formed by rain action during a period when the banks were above water.

The Piri Re'is map and Antonio Zeno map respectively show the landmasses of South America, the Antarctic continent and Greenland, depicting the latter two as ice-free—conditions extant 8,000 to 10,000 years ago. (The maps, Renaissance copies of others said to have been in the library at Alexandria, are a mystery in themselves. No one knows the age of the originals, or who charted them.) Further, analysis of lava samples from the Atlantic floor has revealed that the ocean bottom from which they were collected was above water and volcanically active no later than 10,000 to 15,000 years ago.

Moreover, additional questions rise from the mysterious appearance of Cro-Magnon Man in France, Spain, and America. It was this magnificent creature—with an average adult height of over six feet and a cranial capacity comparable to our own—who replaced the primitive and ungainly Neanderthal Man. With his arrival he brought the skins of a fairly advanced race (witness the cave paintings of Lascaux in France and Altamira in Spain). He did not rely on wood and stone but employed sophisticated and intricate implements of bone, delicately carved, including bone needles with eyes which he used for sewing skins together. He bedecked himself with necklaces and mantles of bone, shell, and teeth. With his carefully fashioned tools he carved ivory; with his clever weapons—including harpoon, and bow and arrow—he hunted; he also domesticated certain animals and cereal grains. These achievements indicate that he had progressed from the state of nomadic wanderer to that of permanent village dweller.

But where did he come from? He already had reached his extraordinary stage of development when he appeared in Spain, France, Greece, and Egypt. He appeared spontaneously—as if from nowhere on earth—and scholars have succeeded in tracing his culture only as far as the Canary Islands. These islands are actually the peaks of a mountain spine extending from the north Atlantic to the northwestern coast of Africa. It is likely that the Canaries are the last remains of a sizable series of submerged islands—perhaps even at one time an entire continent. Equally suggestive is the date Cro-Magnon Man made his debut in Europe. It is estimated at 23,000 B.C., with migratory waves up to 10,000 B.C.—precisely the date fixed by Plato and Cayce for the submergence of Atlantis.

In passing we might note the curious fact that the Basques, a cultural group isolated for innumerable centuries in the Pyrenees, their origins clouded in mystery, still speak a language unlike any other in the Indo-European family. A unique language on the earth, it nonetheless resembles the tongues of some American Indian tribes! Baffled linguistic experts never have considered the possibility that this enigma suggests both groups are linked to a single origin.

If we weigh all of the evidence in the light of reason we still have no more than a hypothesis, albeit a substantial one. But the absence of concrete physical proof does not necessarily preclude the existence of a historical reality; after all, Herodotus was proclaimed history's greatest liar—until Pompeii was uncovered. We must remember too that written history is a mere 5,000 years old and that, prior to written records, historical events survived through an oral tradition. Thus the "legend" of King Arthur remained a fairy tale until recent excavations disclosed the actual site of Camelot.

And so it may be with our Atlantic islands. For the time being the evidence warrants a healthy skepticism—but we would be foolish to deny the possibility that new developments, perhaps in the near future, could clear up forever the many questions surrounding the lost continent. Who knows? Perhaps our generation will find the answer to one of history's riddles.

Other Ocean Oddities

Unidentified Submarine Objects

Martin Caidin
April & May 1995

Nobody knows what they are, or where they're from.

The ocean bottom changes to craggy surfaces and tumbled cliffs, then descends steadily to the Vema Gap, which widens abruptly into the Nares Abyssal Plain off the southeast coast of Florida. Just south of this line lies the enormous cleft of the deep Puerto Rican Trench. It is an area of intense oceanographic study for hydrological measurements, and it is also a great practice area for fleets of warships, submarines, and aircraft to test the science and practice of anti-submarine warfare.

Rear Admiral John S. Thach, USN, describes this area as "a relatively unexplored jungle; whole mountain ranges, deep canyons, and many strange creatures . . . this liquid space is a murky mass of discontinuities, full of sound ducts, currents, and thermal layers. Most incredible of all is the noise racketing through the undersea jungle."

Thirty years ago, in 1964, a powerful anti-submarine warfare fleet (ASW) operated in the testing range area designated as AUTEC, where our military forces were conducting grimly realistic war games of tracking "enemy attack submarines" that were playing the role of slashing at our surface and submarine vessels. Research ships carrying out their own complementary tests were deployed throughout the military task force. The most modern equipment in the world, staffed by experienced technicians, scanned the ocean from the surface to more than five miles down into the sea.

On one vessel, the chief sonar operator suddenly clapped his hands in pain to his earphones, pressing them inward tightly while he stared with disbelief at his instrument panel. Painfully loud sonar pings shrilled into his earphones. He was sonar-tracking the sound of a submarine, driving hard, pounding with enormous energy through the seas. And it was deep. The sonarman and other technicians crowding about his console could hardly believe what they saw and heard. A single mighty screw hammered through the depths with impossible speed, yet they knew their instruments were working perfectly.

Every ship in the research group immediately shut down its engines. All instruments, scientific and military, trained on that great undersea vessel. All their instruments provided a definite, precise crosscheck.

Cruising at Impossible Speeds

That powerful throbbing was coming to them from a depth of 27,000 feet. The many instruments of the fleet confirmed the speed of the object at 120 knots, which was just not possible. At that depth the unknown object was enduring a pressure of nearly two million pounds per square foot.

Immediately the research team contacted two other military ASW fleets also on maneuvers, all of which were out of each other's sight over the horizon. All began tracking. They picked up the unknown vessel at the same depth and speed.

One scientist turned to his associates. "This is like a nightmare. It's crazy. We'll never hear it again," he said.

The next morning, all three fleets, hundreds of miles apart, confirmed the incredible tracking events of the previous day. They tracked the mysterious undersea vessel for several days, until it disappeared.

Five miles deep into the realm of hydrospace, a ship—or some form of life, or maybe even a vessel alien to this planet—performed as easily and swiftly as a jet skimming through air.

To the U.S. Navy and many scientists in the field of oceanography and hydrospace, the less said about mysterious objects racing through the seas, especially objects no one can identify or explain, the better. The *AUTEC Report*, as the incident became known within Congress and the committees that controlled funds for anti-submarine activity, left the Navy and its associated research teams acutely embarrassed. Immediately a connotation was established—because it made good news copy for certain political figures—that the U.S. was wrestling as much with USOs (Unidentified Submarine Objects) as it was with a horde of UFOs that were provoking mass discomfort and near-hysteria in millions of people.

UFOs could be understood—at least in a sense. They flew through the air or in some unknown way were able to float, drift, or levitate. Since there are between 6,000 and 9,000 ordinary aircraft traversing American skies at any one time, there is every reason to expect that people would regard a few of these as something more than winged aircraft, helicopters, or balloons manufactured in American factories.

But it didn't work that way for the considerably more rare unknown things maneuvering through the ocean with a power and agility that made the U.S. (and other) naval forces look like water-logged klutzes.

As a result of several mysterious reports of this type, we—the author and a research team—began investigating incidents of unknown vehicles or creatures that surpassed all known forms of flight, suspension, and performance. None of these occurrences could conveniently be explained. Here follow a few of the fascinating events we uncovered.

Ghost rockets

Right after World War II ended, ghost rockets became the hottest news in the Scandinavian countries, especially Sweden. Dozens of great rockets spewing out brilliant flames were seen rising, falling, and racing across the sky. Investigation proved that these weren't German V-2 rockets left over from the war. There was no other reasonable explanation for these rockets, yet they were witnessed by experienced pilots and military observers who were familiar with rocket vehicles.

Then the occurrences became even more bizarre and the rockets began behaving in impossible ways, violating the capabilities of every known form of rocket or rocket flight. Long-time pilots were startled to see a rocket-shaped device diving steeply toward the surface of Lake Kolmjarv. The rocket slammed into the water, sent up a huge geyser, and disappeared beneath the surface. Moments later a thundering boom issued from within the lake. Observers marked the spot and teams of divers were sent out to find the wreckage of whatever had plowed into the lake, but nothing was ever found.

The observer reports were so exact and the men were so experienced that they couldn't have been mistaken. A search for similar events elsewhere was begun immediately.

Ring-Shaped Flying Craft

Then, in the summer of 1947, six ring-shaped flying craft appeared 2,000 feet above the ocean waters off Tacoma, Washington. The six shapes slowed their flight and finally came to a hover. Five of the objects began to circle the sixth craft, which was now moving erratically, as though out of control. It began a wobbling descent until it was only a few hundred feet over the water. Three men, a boy, and a dog in a boat close to the scene stared at the astonishing sight.

At the time, the boat was close to the shoreline of Maury Island, off the coast of Washington. The men reported the rings as about 100 feet in diameter, each with a central space. They were made of gleaming metal and reflected silver and gold. There were porthole-shaped windows, and each craft had one large observation window.

The witnesses suddenly heard a heavy booming thud. The center craft tore apart as if exploding from within. A shock wave reached the four people in the boat, and silvery pieces rained down onto them and beyond, to the beach. Several pieces struck and injured the boy, ending all question as to the actual physical nature of the event. A heavier piece struck and killed the boy's dog.

Several men on shore, unrelated to the men in the boat, were there for a filming venture that was never identified, and they filmed the incredible events. Soon after, as word of the bizarre events spread, the men with the film were approached by another man who identified himself as an official with the government, and asked for the film to study. There was no reason to withhold the film, especially after a solemn promise to return the developed film once a copy was made—but the man was never seen again, the film was never returned, and the government professed complete ignorance of the entire matter.

The debris from the exploded ring was collected by the men on the shore and the distraught men and boy in the boat. They described it as resembling slag ash. Air Force officers suddenly appeared and collected the ash. They offhandedly said it was very similar to volcanic rock. Their seeming disinterest was soon contradicted by uniformed air force intelligence officers who landed at a nearby field in a B-25 bomber, collected a box of debris, and took off east the next day.

Twenty minutes later the B-25 exploded, although the crew had not reported any problems. Two enlisted men bailed out and parachuted to safety, but an intelligence officer and several other men were officially reported as having died in the explosion.

To my knowledge, no one has ever made sense of or explained this episode. There were witnesses to the bizarre craft, films of the event, witnesses to the explosion, an injured youth, a dead dog, and an unexplained appearance by military and other officials—yet the story vanished amid denials and contradictions perpetrated by the government.

A History of Sightings

The bizarre reports of submersible objects go well back in time. In May 1880, the steamship *Patna* of the British India

Company cruised through the Persian Gulf. At midnight the crewman on watch shouted hysterically to the officers on the bridge. Two luminous wheels, described as "absolutely gigantic," were rushing alongside the *Patna*. Long spokes from one glowing wheel seemed to be actually slamming into the steamship, but no one, including those watching closely, heard or felt any impacts. Then, abruptly, the luminous wheels increased their speed and the crew heard a deep swishing sound. For twenty minutes all hands on deck and on the bridge of the steamship kept the objects in view, until they finally moved far ahead of the *Patna* and disappeared in the distance. No one could explain what had been witnessed by almost the entire crew.

Over the next several years, other stories were recorded, and the reports became ever more bizarre, even with hundreds of experienced and reliable witnesses. One such event took place above and within the waters of Lake Erie. Several men crewing a boat captained by Joseph Singler sighted an odd-looking vessel well ahead of them. Singler headed for the unknown craft, and, as they approached the strange boat, a huge balloon expanded almost instantly above the vessel.

One moment it wasn't there; then it snapped into being to a height of at least 600 feet. What came next defies all sense and logic, especially to the men with Captain Singler. An enormous swordfish appeared to be ejected violently from the balloon-borne boat, and with unerring accuracy smashed with terrific force into Singler's craft! The unidentified vessel, whatever it was, then sailed away through the sky, diminishing steadily in size as it accelerated away from Singler's ship. The men on board could hardly believe what they had experienced—except that the dead swordfish was still there.

A Torpedo-Shaped Craft

On July 30, 1967, the Argentine steamship *Naviero* cruised in the South Atlantic, a little more than 100 miles off the coast of Brazil. It was one of the more pleasant times of day and the majority of the crew was at dinner. The weather was pleasant and the ship rolled easily and comfortably.

Suddenly, Jorge Montoya, bridge duty officer, began shouting into the intercom that led to the officers' mess. Looking starboard, Montoya stared in near-shock at a large, torpedo-shaped craft moving steadily beneath the ocean surface. It was clearly visible and pacing the *Naviero,* only fifty feet away. It maintained its position with the *Naviero* for fifteen minutes. It had been glowing softly, but abruptly the light intensified to a blinding, bluish white light. More than 100 feet long, it left no wake and not so much as a ripple in the sea, despite its bulk and speed.

Then all hell broke loose. The mystery shape turned directly toward the merchantman, accelerated rapidly, and glowed with a dazzling light. Just before striking the ship, it dove beneath the *Naviero.* As it passed beneath the ship, the crew rushed to the opposite deck to watch the brilliant shape speeding away, deeper and faster.

Late at night on July 26, 1980, a tugboat, the *Caioba-Seahorse,* closed in on an unidentified object floating in the sea about sixty miles off the Brazilian coast. The first mate on watch looked up as a bright light came into view and then descended swiftly. The officer had to turn his vessel to avoid striking the object, estimated at thirty feet in diameter and still floating on the surface. Suddenly the floating object "exploded silently" in wild and shifting colors. The object was still the same shape, but it flashed colors in rapid succession.

Then a UFO came clearly into view well above the sea. It was oval-shaped and shining brilliantly. It hovered directly above the floating, multi-colored object, then sank slowly toward the sea.

The two objects made solid contact and then rose into the air as a single craft. The USO lights winked out, and the combined ship floated in the air silently before putting on a sudden burst of speed and accelerating upward until it was out of sight. What was even more amazing is that no one on the *Caioba-Seahorse* even tried to figure out what it was all about!

Fast Takes

John Gallagher was hard at work at Newport, Rhode Island, in April 1961 when sudden activity off the shore caught his attention. A glowing red ball or sphere of some type bobbed in choppy water. With unexpected motion, the sphere shot higher than fifty feet, came to a dead stop, shot forward at 100 miles per hour, and maintained this speed in an absolutely direct line to the east, until it dwindled to a speck and was lost from sight.

On April 13, 1964, "All hell broke loose," reported a witness aboard a bus in London, when a long, streamlined UFO plunged from the sky above the River Lea. It came down without regard to obstructions, smashed through telephone wires, ripped a huge gouge in a concrete bank, and walloped into a river that was only about seven feet deep. What no one could explain was how a craft much larger than seven feet could have disappeared within the river. Local authorities discounted what the drivers and passengers had seen, with the explanation that they really had watched a flight of ducks descending. But no one could explain how the ducks became silvery metallic, slashed telephone wires, and ripped up concrete. The police refused comment.

In March 1965, several pilots flying over the St. Lawrence River in Canada looked down from their airliner at a large submarine in the river, 200 miles from the ocean. Experienced in aerial observation and on a schedule, the pilots reported the submarine and flew on. Canadian authorities coldly denied any such vessel was ever in the river.

Several years later, in May 1969, several witnesses saw a "great round shining thing in the sky, with very bright flashing red lights. It flew straight toward the St. Lawrence River and suddenly dove into the river at great speed." All further details were blocked by local authorities.

A sighting by nearly 100 people waiting for a ferry on the Araguari River of Brazil was made in November 1980. The crowd gaped at a fifty-foot object rising steadily from the river. The object rose to 700 feet, turned in a circle, and drifted seaward until it was out of sight.

Somewhat more violent was a sighting in May 1981, when a man fishing the Thompson River of British Columbia saw nearby water boiling with sudden white fury. Out of the cascading foam a huge object slid smoothly from the river, hovered briefly, and then tore away upward until lost to sight.

North of New York City, near the Titicus reservoir, two people watched a glowing, luminous sphere illuminate the water, brighten steadily, and turn a deep pink. The sphere lunged from the water and then fell back with a thunderous splash. Hours later the lake seemed to froth and boil. A dark object shot upward from beneath the surface. Horizontal light streaks and a thin yellow light revolved at the object's peak, which hovered over the lake for hours. In the morning it was gone.

Many More Accounts

Even these few reports strain the imagination, but so did the first moon landings, which are now absolutely believed by millions of people. There are many more accounts reported by reliable witnesses from all over the world.

Many of the almost-mystical sightings at sea have come from frightened sailors who were forced to accept the reality of what their senses told them—in defiance of everything they had ever been told was possible and/or logical.

But there have been enough documented sightings of so-called oceanic UFOs to eliminate all questions about their appearance. They are absolutely, unquestionably luminous, they range from twenty feet to nearly 2,000 feet in size, and they have been seen both without crews and with humanoid figures aboard them. They travel both above and below the surface of the ocean, and they apparently have some strange purpose in diving into rivers and lakes.

And nobody knows what they are, or where they're from.

I Found God's Island

Barbara Falk
November 1964

Food, furniture, paint, wood—whatever is needed on this tiny isle appears to be miraculously supplied.

Sixteen years ago while I was ill with the flu I dreamed a beautiful dream. This dream—which literally changed my life—showed me an island, an emerald green dot in a blue sapphire sea, with sparkling waves washing onto a white shore.

For a few months I continued to live haunted by that dream; it became absolutely overpowering. I resigned my office position, sold my home in Maryland, and bought a ticket to Florida. I had no idea where I was going. I was following a dream, and I had faith. Somehow I wound up in Gulfport.

Reaching the shore I gazed across the choppy water of Boco Ceiga Bay toward the Gulf of Mexico, silently seeing for the first time the tiny green islands dotting the horizon.

As I turned to leave the shore I saw a sixteen-foot boat for sale. Although not fancy, it looked sturdy enough and the price was about what I could pay.

I loaded my boat with provisions and headed out toward the green dots. I did not worry about where I was going, and rightly, for when it was almost sunset I recognized my dream island.

It lay under a reddening sky in all its serene natural beauty, and on October 12, 1948, Columbus Day, I landed on it.

Pitching my tent among the bayonet plants that were in full white bloom I felt I had entered the Garden of Eden. Within a few days I had built a cozy little house out of driftwood and thick thatch made from palm fronds.

Never had I felt so close to God. I spoke aloud to Him, thanking Him for leading me to this precious paradise. It did not occur to me the island might be owned by someone else; I took it for granted it belonged to me and to God.

With some concern I eventually left my island to see the state authorities, and it was with awe at the wondrous ways of God that I learned my island somehow had escaped the state survey and did not show on official maps. If I would have the island surveyed, I was free to claim it.

I am told the island is about 250 years old, which means it was being created for me long before I was born. I sent in all the money I had to pay expenses, but I still was $200 short. I promised to send the remainder in a few days, and I didn't worry about how I would get it. I said, "Dear Jesus, I know You will take care of me."

Exactly four days later a man came ashore in a rowboat and asked if he might take pictures of me and the island for his magazine. He offered me $200. I never saw the pictures or the story, but I did get the money I needed to become the island's first owner since its creation by God.

Throughout the years God has remained with me on our island, watching over me and ministering to my needs. One time when my provisions almost were depleted, a squall lasting several days prevented me from either going to the mainland or from going fishing. Looking up at the heavens, where low, dark clouds drifted by, I said aloud, "Dear God, I wish I had fish for supper."

At that instant there was a splash. I looked toward the sound and saw something dive into my boat. It was a mullet.

One day I laughed when I realized I had two bunks but no chair. The next morning a big garden chair floated in to the island from the gulf. Another time I wished for a bamboo fishing pole, and the next morning I found it in my boat.

A few months later I returned from Pass-a-grille Beach on the mainland with my mail just before sundown, when the tide was almost out. As I sat in my house reading my letter and munching a snack, I heard something hit the window screen across the room, and I caught a glimpse of a falling bird. My glance then fell to the floor. Less than a foot and a half away a rattlesnake was crawling toward me. Quickly I got on my bunk, reached for my rifle, and killed it.

Who but God could have sent that bird at the exact instant I needed to be warned of the menace on the floor? One more second and I would have finished my letter and surely stepped on the snake.

I was reared a Christian, but not until I came to this island had I believed God was so close and so miraculous. I tacked to my wall a piece of paper with the words, "It's so nice living alone with God."

Hal Boyle of International Press visited me and God's Island several years ago. He quoted those words in a column.

Ten years ago I married retired Colonel Donald Falk, and then there were two of us on the island. I told him of all the miracles God had worked. He thought it was wonderful, but his faith truly deepened when these awesome coincidences began happening to him.

One day last year I was making a jetty to catch sand, but I needed a few more driftwood boards. My husband had two, but he needed them for something he was making.

Since I lacked the materials, I went inside to take care of some housework.

About an hour later my husband called me outside. He pointed toward the gulf and asked, "What is that large thing floating here fast?" It landed in the cove and wedged itself in among the weeds.

The object was a fifteen-foot square, three-ply raft-like structure. Heaped in the center like a tepee were all types and sizes of lumber. There also was a can of copper screws.

It was as if an unseen hand had pushed it, because that day there was hardly a breeze. Here was more than enough lumber for my jetty.

Another time, as they walked along the shore, my husband described to a Christian friend some of the wonderful things that had happened. The friend was skeptical and changed the subject. "Don, when are you going to finish painting your boat?"

"After payday," my husband answered. "I have to go to town to get more paint."

They walked on farther, until our friend pointed to a gallon can on the shore and remarked, "Wonder what's in it." He kicked it and it was heavy. The two men picked it up and brought it back to my husband's workshop.

The can contained paint—gray paint, the exact shade of gray with which the boat had been partially painted. Our friend was convinced.

The Deadly Mermaid Pool

Ruth Bennett
April 1981

As he stared into the water his face turned blank and suddenly we realized he was about to jump.

On the moors in Derbyshire, England, daylight arrives late, stays a few hours, then surrenders to an early dusk. Even in midsummer the watery sun seldom penetrates the mists shrouding the high hills. This is fertile ground for stories of the supernatural—and this is one of them.

In August 1956 my parents James and Margaret Webb and I were staying with friends named Woods on their farmstead near Elkstone. It was the last week of the summer holiday. Soon we would be going home to Wellingborough, Northamptonshire, and I would be returning to school.

The Woodses' farm was called "Mount Pleasant" and it was rumored that the old rambling farmhouse contained a secret passage. Sylvia Woods, the farmer's daughter who was about my age, and I had searched diligently for more than a week but we found nothing more than cobwebs, spiders, a toad or two, and once s badger hibernating in the basement. When our flashlights awakened this temporary lodger he was not pleased. Sylvia grabbed my arm and I jumped.

"Quiet, silly," she giggled. "It's only me. Come on. We have yet to collect the eggs."

Collecting eggs is not the most difficult chore—unless you're on a farm in Derbyshire. Here the farmers allow their hens to wander where they will which means they lay their eggs wherever they happen to be. Sylvia and I were late in starting our egg hunt and in the gathering dusk we wandered apart. I had partially filled my basket when a shadow seemed to appear in front of me. I started back in alarm and bumped into Sylvia who was looking intently at her watch.

Quietly she told me, "We'll have to hurry. We're right in his path."

"Whose path?" Sylvia was starting down the hill.

"The headless horseman." She threw the words over her shoulder. "He'll be riding out here very shortly."

Shivering and shaking I called out, "Wait for me," as I raced after her. In my haste to escape the menace I felt drawing closer I bypassed Sylvia and we reached the house together—where we were scolded for not going for the eggs earlier.

The Mermaid's Tale

In the cozy farmhouse lighted by candles and a kerosene lamp my fears were soon forgotten. After a traditional dinner of homegrown vegetables (moor people rarely eat meat), apple pie, and thick rich cream, I asked Mr. Woods to tell us a legend of the moors. He lit his pipe as we pulled up our chairs and gathered around the stove.

"At the top of the highest of all the moors," Sylvia's father began in a deep pleasant voice, "there is a bottomless pool which legend says is the home of a mermaid. At night she rises and any man in the vicinity is drawn by her hypnotic eyes to the pool where he drowns."

"Has this happened?" my mother asked.

"Indeed it has," said Mr. Woods. "Only last spring old Mr. Marsh disappeared on his way home from the market. Next morning the tracks of his horse and cart were found leading to the pool. This was all reported in the weekly paper from Leek." Mrs. Woods produced the clipping and showed it to Mother.

"But couldn't he have just been lost and taken the wrong route, falling into the pool by mistake?" inquired my father.

Mr. Woods looked at him for a long time. Then he arose, added some wood to the stove, and said, "Indeed he could have—but he didn't." To Sylvia and me he said pointedly, "Good night, children."

In our room I asked Sylvia, "Why couldn't he have fallen in? How do any of you know he didn't lose his way?"

Sylvia looked at me in much the same way as her father had looked at my father. "There's a fence," she said. "The horse and cart disappeared and they couldn't have fallen in. Old Mr. Marsh would have had to climb the fence. You tell me why he would do that."

I shivered—but I wasn't satisfied, I had to see for myself. When Mother came in to say good night I whispered, "I'd like to see that pool."

"So would I," she answered. "Go to sleep now. I'll talk to your father."

Seeing Is Believing

The mermaid pool was about eight miles across the moors from Elkstone off the road from Leek to Buxton. After breakfast the next morning, when my parents announced their intention of visiting the pool, Mrs. Woods turned pale. Her husband said only, "Make sure you're back before dusk."

Dad nodded and went to get his camera. When he returned he was wearing a quilted plastic raincoat. "The mist is heavy," he said. "You'll need raincoats and galoshes."

A little later we started out. Almost two hours later we reached the top of the moor and stared down into the awesome depths of the murky mermaid pool.

Try to imagine yourself on a high hill, the daylight fading, a misty rain falling, all the legends of the moors running through your mind, and you may sense the chills that assailed me as I looked into the pool.

My father and I were standing at the fence and Mother a little ways off was adjusting the camera. Suddenly she called me to move away. She said, "Jim, look down as if you were looking for a mermaid."

As she finished speaking, a wind arose from nowhere, grabbed at Dad's raincoat and pulled it from his shoulders. It flew into the center of the pool and began to sink slowly, one part at a time. My father, white as a sheet, was watching the raincoat disappear. He had one foot on the fence and, as we watched in horror, he turned toward the pool and put his other foot on the wooden bars as if to climb over.

I screamed, "Daddy, Daddy!" and Mother and I with one accord raced toward him. Mother grabbed his arm and cried, "Come on, Jim! That mermaid's after you."

Dad turned, his face blank. Never have I seen such an expression as his and never again do I want to. It seemed as if he had left us and gone somewhere we couldn't follow. I took his other arm and we led him away from the pool. He shook his head and slowly, very slowly, seemed to recognize us. Then we all fairly flew down the hill. At the bottom we found a welcome sight: Mr. Woods in his pony trap.

"Thought I'd better come looking for you," he said. We climbed gratefully into the cart. Dad was shivering.

"There's hot tea under the seat and an extra blanket. Wrap him up and give him some drink at once," Mr. Woods said. Half-turning, he looked sternly at us. "At once!" he repeated as he turned the cart homeward.

My father is no coward. As a master sergeant in the British army he was in charge of a squadron of gunners during World War II and many a time they faced death. But when we reached the farmhouse he said, "I don't mind admitting I was scared."

When told of the day's events Mrs. Woods said just two words: "You're lucky."

Miracles at Sea

Harvey Berman

March 1958

The series of disasters was strange enough—but even stranger, they seem to have been arranged for a single purpose.

On a blustery October morning in 1829 the schooner *Mermaid* set sail from Sydney, Australia, for Collier Bay on the west coast of the continent. Captain Samuel Nolbrow was at the wheel and there were eighteen seamen and three passengers aboard. Rarely have twenty-two sea-going souls been subjected to greater privations or caught up in a more fantastic chain of events than these people. The series of incidents that followed their setting sail defy the imagination and are probably without parallel in the history of humans against the sea.

For three days the *Mermaid* followed her course without mishap. The wind was fair. The sky was clear. The glass was steady. Sydney was far astern when Captain Nolbrow went below, as he usually did during the uneventful voyage around northern Australia, leaving his vessel in charge of his second in command. The crew, for their part—once the skipper had gone to keep company with his "wee little Scotties" contained in a case of good English whiskey purchased just before sailing time—lolled about the deck basking in the sun, and attending to their few duties.

On the fourth day out, however, the wind died down abruptly and an uneasy silence fell over the becalmed *Mermaid.* The quiet and the lack of motion suddenly wrenched a red-nosed Nolbrow out of his stupor and back to the helm of his schooner. On deck he noticed that the barometer was falling and that the sky was a sullen wall of darkness. His crew stood idly by, waiting for whatever was coming.

Shortly before midnight—when the *Mermaid* was in Torres Strait, a treacherous body of water separating Australia and New Guinea and strewn with a thousand and one traps for a ship—the storm hit. High winds ripped through the schooner's rigging and hurled mammoth waves over her starboard rail. Hard rain beat down relentlessly. Frantically, Nolbrow watched the *Mermaid* being driven toward a ridge of rocks to the north. Desperately he attempted to stave off disaster. Nothing, however, would turn the ship from its storm-driven course, from its rendezvous with destruction.

Three hours after the storm first hit the *Mermaid* struck a coral reef. With a hiss and an impact that rocked the vessel, her bottom was ripped away and the angry sea poured into her hold.

"Abandon ship," Nolbrow ordered.

Disorganized seamen and passengers hurled themselves over the side and started swimming toward an immense rock jutting out of the water about 200 feet downwind. In the panic and the darkness it seemed certain that the loss of life would be heavy. Yet, later, when the exhausted Captain Nolbrow pulled himself up onto the rock—he was the last to abandon his ship—a count revealed that all twenty-two people aboard the *Mermaid* had made it to safety. Incredible but true—not a single life had been lost in the violent sea that had sunk the *Mermaid*.

Three days elapsed before help arrived. Finally, the boat *Swiftsure* came into view and picked up the *Mermaid*'s survivors. Continuing on her course, the *Swiftsure* headed west.

But disaster struck for the second time. Passing close to New Guinea, the *Swiftsure* found herself caught up in an overpowering current—a current that was not indicated on any of the excellent charts of the area. And the *Swiftsure* was dashed to pieces against rocks which jutted out along the coastline. Again the order "abandon ship" was given. This time two crews abandoned ship—the survivors of the ill-fated *Mermaid* and their rescuers from the *Swiftsure*. And again, all aboard were safe.

Aid was not long in coming this time. That very same day the *Governor Ready*, with a crew of thirty-two, sailed over the horizon. The castaways were taken aboard the schooner and the *Governor Ready* clapped on sail and resumed her trip, sailing to disaster even faster than the *Mermaid* and the *Swiftsure*. Only hours after the rescue the schooner caught fire and three sets of survivors lowered the *Governor Ready*'s longboats and rowed for safety. Around them lay hundreds of miles of water—a vast expanse through which few vessels traveled. The outlook was not bright. Nevertheless, by some miracle, the government cutter *Comet* appeared. A storm had blown her off course. Sighting the exhausted seamen she headed for them. By evening all survivors had been taken aboard.

Three ships lay at the bottom of the sea and not a single life had been lost. The crews and passengers of the *Mermaid*, *Swiftsure*, and *Governor Ready* were all aboard the *Comet*, hungry, weary, but alive.

For a week all went well. But the *Mermaid*'s crew, believing they must have had a Jonah among them, was strangely silent. The crew of the *Swiftsure* huddled in one corner while the seamen of the *Governor Ready* sat in still another place. The *Comet*'s sailors, meanwhile, shunned the company of all three crews, looking upon their guests with uneasy suspicion. Their fears, as subsequent events proved, were justified, A sudden storm blew up and by the time the winds and the rain subsided the *Comet* was a doomed ship. Four crews now took to the water. The men aboard the *Comet* launched a longboat, while the other three crews floundered in the violent sea, desperately attempting to keep afloat on odds and ends of wreckage.

Eighteen hours passed in this fashion, hours of fighting the cold sea and the hungry sharks that circled the floundering men. Hope was nearly gone when the *Jupiter* came and rescued the exhausted sailors from what had seemed certain death. When the captains of the four lost vessels checked their men they discovered that for the fourth time all hands bad been saved. Somehow, despite four successive disasters, the complete companies of four sunken vessels—every last man of them—were still together, still alive.

Yet, the misfortunes of the *Mermaid*'s crew and the four crews that had rescued them were not over. Two days from port the *Jupiter* struck a reef and sank. This time the *City Of Leeds* was nearby. A rescue was quickly accomplished and the *City Of Leeds* continued towards her destination.

Now misfortune of another sort appeared. This time a passenger, an elderly Englishwoman, fell gravely ill. Dr. Thomas Sparks, a physician on one of the ships, gave her only a few hours to live.

During these last hours there was only one thing that the woman wanted. Delirious, she called constantly for her son, a boy she had not seen since he ran away to join the Royal Navy, nearly fifteen years before. Finally, coming up on deck, Dr. Sparks cast about for a sailor who would match the age and general appearance of the vanished youth the patient spoke about. He found a perfect substitute among the crew of the *Mermaid.* Thirty years old with blue eyes and dark hair, the man even had been born in England. Moreover, when asked to help the young man proved willing to deceive the elderly woman so that she might die in peace.

Together, the doctor and the seaman went below. Outside the woman's cabin the physician turned to his accomplice and told him what he must do.

"Listen carefully, lad," he said. "The poor woman's name is Sarah Richley. I want you to pretend that you're her son, Peter. Got that? Remember the name—Peter Richley—don't make a mistake."

The sailor was no longer listening. His face had turned white and he leaned against the wall in the narrow companionway. Sparks looked at him in astonishment.

"There, boy, what's the matter?" he asked. "Don't tell me you've lost your stomach for this act of mercy."

The seaman, barely able to talk, whispered, "I needn't repeat the name you gave me, Dr. Sparks. I mean . . . I mean . . . that I won't forget it. You see, sir, my name is Peter Richley, and the old woman you say is dying in there must be my mother, who I haven't seen since I left Yorkshire fifteen years ago come this Whitsunday."

Thus one good circumstance came of this amazing saga of disaster on the high seas. Fate had brought together Sarah and Peter Richley even though it had sacrificed five vessels to do it. At the same time not a single life had been lost. All of the five captains were cited for valor and advanced in rank. All of the cargo destroyed was covered by insurance. It appears the insurance companies paid for Fate's whim.

Further, the reunion achieved more than the doctor had expected of it. Mrs. Richley was so happy to see her son that her condition immediately took a turn for the better. As a matter of fact, she lived for nearly twenty years more, in a house her long-lost son built for her in Sydney.

Captain Robson's Lost Island

William L. Moore
July 1985

The island rose out of the ocean, revealed evidence of a past civilization—then vanished without a trace.

Once past the Madeira Islands, the shipping lanes between the Straits of Gibraltar and the Gulf of Mexico are a lonely place, for beyond that point lies nothing but several thousand miles of empty, windswept Atlantic. Over the years many strange stories have been told about mysterious happenings in that stretch of ocean. Perhaps the strangest concerns the reported experience of Captain David Amory Robson, master of the steamship *Jesmond*, when he chanced across that area of water more than a century ago.

For many hundreds of years that particular expanse has been rumored to be the watery resting place of a legendary ancient civilization. Although geological evidence seems to indicate that at least parts of the area must have been above water, in the last 10,000 to 20,000 years, no one has ever found anything sufficiently conclusive to challenge the conventional wisdom that holds Atlantis to be no more than a curiously tenacious myth. There is, however, the strange story of Captain Robson, who may or may not have found the proof that has eluded so many for so long.

David A. Robson was born in South Shields, England, on October 20, 1839. He was the holder of Ship's Master's Certificate No. 27911 in the British Merchant Marine and was already an experienced seafarer when in the latter part of 1881 he drew command of the S.S. *Jesmond*, a 1,945-ton steamer owned by Watts, Watts & Co. of Threadneedle Street in London.

The winter of 1882 saw the *Jesmond* enjoying the warmth of various Mediterranean ports. Then on February 22, it departed Messina with a cargo of dried fruits destined for New Orleans on what all assumed would be a leisurely five-week voyage.

By March 1, the *Jesmond* had cleared Gibraltar. Following the trade routes, it continued its southwesterly voyage uneventfully past the Madeiras and the Canaries and out into the open Atlantic. It was at about latitude 26 degrees north and longitude 22 degrees west that the first indications of something out of the ordinary appeared.

Robson thought it strange that the usually clear seawater of the area had suddenly taken on a dark, murky appearance.

His puzzlement gave way to concern when the *Jesmond* came upon thick masses of recently dead fish. All night long, mile after mile, the ship plowed through the carpet of fish. Finally, curious but tiring of the sight, Robson retired for the night, leaving orders to be awakened immediately if there was any change in the situation.

His second officer's frantic pounding on the door early the next morning brought word of just such a change. Either the man was crazy or land had been sighted dead ahead. Robson rushed to the bridge, rubbed his eyes and stared in astonishment. There, where the charts indicated nothing but 2,000 fathoms of saltwater, was a new and uncharted island, complete with several lofty and still smoking peaks!

Fearful of reefs, Robson ordered speed reduced to a near-crawl and began taking precautionary soundings. Almost at once the lead registered bottom at a mere 300 feet. The captain could hardly conceal his confusion. The pervasive odor of dead fish, the sight of an island where there should have been none and now a sea bottom of 300 feet where there should have been 12,000 all worked to convince him that either he was no longer on Earth or something extraordinary had occurred.

Proceeding cautiously and continuing to take soundings, Robson guided the *Jesmond* toward the mountainous apparition. At about ten miles from shore, Robson decided not to risk his ship in the increasingly shallow water which now registered only slightly more than forty feet deep and was getting shallower. He stopped all engines and dropped anchor. Quickly a boat was put over the side and Robson, accompanied by a third officer and a landing party, set off to explore the unknown.

As he made his way slowly along the lower western side of the island, he found himself facing a large flat expanse of what appeared to be volcanic debris stretching inland toward a high plateau some miles away. Beyond this he could see peaks of distant volcanoes. The area seemed arid and devoid of life. Unable to find anything resembling a beach—a fact that in itself indicated the island couldn't have been there for any length of time—Robson directed his boat to what seemed to be a bed of coarse gravel fronting the shoreline.

The men scrambled ashore to view a landscape that might as well have been on the moon. Although Robson ordered his men to keep together, efforts to explore any distance inland from the rocky shore were repeatedly blocked by a hodgepodge of pumice, huge boulders and deep crevasses, some emitting thin columns of steam.

Eventually the party returned to the graveled area to decide what ought to be done next. While waiting for the captain's decision, one of the sailors began nervously picking around in the rocks with the tip of his boat hook. To his amazement he turned up a flint arrowhead. This touched off a general search of the area and sailors were sent running to fetch picks and shovels from the longboat. Soon the workers uncovered the ruins of two massive stone walls; between them was an opening leading to a rubble-filled interior.

For the rest of that day and all of the next Robson's men busily excavated and transported to the *Jesmond* a fantastic collection of artifacts and treasures, including bronze spearheads, short cross-hilted swords, rings, hammers, various stone implements, a pair of large spherical wide-mouthed vases carved with birds and animals and inscribed with strange hieroglyphics, an array of bones with a nearly complete skull, and, incredibly, what seemed to be a mummified body in a large stone sarcophagus encrusted with small shells.

That night Robson wrestled with an agonizing decision. His natural impulse was to stay on and investigate further. Unfortunately the weather was worsening noticeably and he already had a two-day delay to make up. At last, realizing his first duty was to his employers, Robson decided there was nothing to be done but carefully note the island's position (latitude 25 degrees north, longitude 23 degrees, 40 minutes west) and sail on to New Orleans with his cargo in the hope of being able to visit the place again on the return trip to England.

Robson Makes News

According the *New Orleans Times-Democrat* for April 2, 1882, the *Jesmond* docked in New Orleans and was in port seven days. Records indicate it "crossed the bar" into New Orleans harbor at 7:30 A.M., March 31. Noon the next day found the ship tied up at "Post 14, First District," at the foot of Erato Street, where it began to unload its cargo into the warehouses of A. B. French & Co.

During the unloading Robson went ashore for a drink and a few moments of much-needed relaxation. While ensconced at a wharfside tavern table with a glass of rum, Robson was approached by the "Marine Intelligence" reporter of the *New Orleans Daily Picayune* and asked how his recent crossing had gone. The reporter must have been more than a little surprised to hear what Robson had to tell him.

The result of the interview appeared in the next morning's *Picayune* as a lengthy article under headlines proclaiming: "A tale of the sea. Interesting narrative of a steamship captain. A strange island and relics of an ancient people discovered."

The substance of the interview was reported in at least eleven other newspapers across the country ranging from the prestigious *Chicago Times*, the *New York Sun*, and the *St. Louis Globe Democrat* to the obscure *Odebolt* [Iowa] *Reporter*. The story inspired such a flood of mail from all over the country that on

April 23, the *Picayune* issued a disclaimer in which it dismissed the whole affair as "an April Fool story."

The April Fool explanation has some degree of credibility in light of the facts surrounding a seemingly related item which appeared under a "Maritime" news heading in a different section of the same newspaper. According to this item, datelined "New York, March 31," One Captain James Newdick of the steamer *Westbourne* arrived in New York from Marseilles, France, that same day and reported "having sighted a new volcanic island about latitude 25 degrees north and [longitude] 24 degrees west" (*Picayune*, April 1).

Although this appears to confirm Captain Robson's story from an entirely independent source (indeed so much so that other writers picked it up and incorporated it into their own coverage of the tale without bothering to check further), a search of the New York newspaper files for the period in question uncovered the truth. These records indeed confirm the arrival of Captain Newdick (variously spelled "Dick" and "Neudick") aboard the 275-foot, 1,886-ton steam schooner *Westbourne* at the Port of New York on March 31, after a "stormy crossing." But beyond that the attendant facts do not support the *Daily Picayune*'s account in any way.

In fact, a front-page story in the April 1, 1882, edition of the *New York Star* titled "Heavy Weather at Sea" not only fails to mention the discovery of any new island but tells quite a different story. According to this account, the *Westbourne*'s last port of call had been Newport, England, not Marseilles, France. It apparently had left Newport on March 10 (although this is reported elsewhere as March 8), accomplished a direct crossing in twenty-one days (thus limited mostly to the 40- to 50-degree latitude belt) and was nearly sunk twice by severe mid-Atlantic storms. One of these storms, the article notes, was encountered at latitude 48 degrees north, longitude 44 degrees west.

Given these facts, we can only conclude that the *Daily Picayune*'s report of Captain Newdick's confirmation of an uncharted island at 25 degrees, 30 minutes north latitude, 24 degrees west longitude, amounts to nothing less than a deliberate fabrication and goes a long way toward discrediting the entire affair. Unfortunately both Newdick and the *Westbourne* were lost in a shipwreck in 1890 and a search for any surviving logbooks has proven futile.

In line with the hoax possibility we must also note that, while the arrival, activities, and departure of the *Jesmond* are duly recorded by the *Picayune*'s rival newspaper the *Times-Democrat* (in editions for April 1, 2, 5, 7 and 8), no mention of Robson's mysterious island was made in any of these. Indeed, the *Times-Democrat* for April 2, records only that the *Jesmond*'s voyage from "Messina via Palermo and Gibraltar" had been "all ordinary passage." Both the *Picayune* and the *Times-Democrat* record that Captain Robson sailed from New Orleans on April 6. He arrived in London on May 19, with a cargo of phosphate taken on at Coosaw, South Carolina.

As for Robson's Island, if it ever existed at all outside the realm of an April Fool's joke, its existence must have been brief indeed. At least, no other mention of such a place has ever been discovered in the annals of the Atlantic sealanes for 1882.

Yet, curiously, some parts of the Robson/*Picayune* story hold up under investigation. Other ships, for example, did encounter the same murky sea and the same carpet of dead fish as did the *Jesmond*. Indeed, numerous accounts mention that ships sailed through huge masses of dead fish and they describe the stench of the rotting mess when it washed up on America's eastern seaboard several weeks later. One ship reported sailing for eleven hours through a solid mass of floating bodies nearly seventy miles wide, only to be outdone by a report from the British Institute of Oceanography which estimated that some

7,500 square miles of Atlantic was covered with over half a million tons of dead fish.

Professor S. F. Baird of the U.S. Fisheries Commission identified many of the fish as members of the genus Lopholatilus (tilefish). Baird theorized that either the fish had been killed when undersea volcanic activity heated the waters, or an exceptionally fierce mid-Atlantic storm had been responsible for the deaths. The reported locations of these carpets of dead fish, however, were generally somewhat more north and west of the location given for Robson's island; yet they are close enough that Robson's claims cannot be dismissed out of hand.

One other piece of supporting evidence is to be found in the navigational charts of the area. While late nineteenth-century charts generally report a uniform depth of about 2,000 fathoms in the vicinity of Robson's reported island, soundings taken during an updating of charts following World War II produced quite different results. In 1954, at a spot closely approximating Robson's reported coordinates and about 100 miles north of the Great Meteor Bank (which itself was discovered only in 1927), an extensive new undersea bank was reported with an average depth of only 11 fathoms (66 feet). Both banks are located on exactly the same extensive volcanic fault as the Azores—islands long associated with the Atlantis legends—and both are considered likely spots by modern geologists for the sort of up-and-down island Robson and his crew reported. If Robson fabricated his story, he certainly picked the right spot. It hardly need be said that nineteenth-century geology had no way of knowing any of this.

Fact or Fake?

But then, why fake such a story in the first place? History shows that Robson never attempted to profit by it. Nor does publicity appear to have been the motive; if it was, how do we explain both Robson's and the *Picayune*'s failure to capitalize on the interest generated by the paper's initial account—especially in light of the fact that the *Picayune* was then engaged in an intense circulation battle with the *Times-Democrat*?

If the story was so patently false, one would think the *Times-Democrat* would have jumped on the matter as a convenient way to heap ridicule on its rival. The two newspapers were battling each other over the issue of which had the larger circulation. Indeed, on April 2, 1882, the *Times-Democrat* challenged the *Picayune* to "wager $10,000 to settle the issue." No mention was made, though, of the *Picayune*'s publishing phony stories—either then or later that same month after the *Picayune*'s "April Fool" statement appeared.

We should also consider that Captain Robson could hardly have endeared himself to his employers in London by reporting a nonexistent island in the middle of a shipping lane. That kind of activity could only have led the firm to question not just his sanity but also his right to further employment. If the story was a fake, then from the standpoint of both his career and his reputation, Robson would clearly have been a fool to be party to it.

But sad to say, the remaining evidence that can be offered in support of Robson's story is sparse indeed. A search for the *Jesmond*'s logbook instituted by British writer L. D. Hills during the early 1950s drew a blank when Hills learned that the document was lost when the offices of the ship's owners were firebombed during the London blitz in the fall of 1940. At the same time inquiries made to Lloyd's of London served only to confirm that the *Jesmond* was indeed once a merchant ship, that Captain Robson was once its master and that the vessel had indeed sailed to New Orleans during the period in question.

Robson's hometown was listed as Jarrow in the county of Durham. Hills instituted an extensive search of antique and curio shops in the area in the slim hope of uncovering a clue to the fate of the presumed artifacts. Durham, Ireland, is a conservative area and antique dealers sometimes have long memories; even so, nothing turned up.

If there ever were any relics and any truth to Robson's reported desire to turn them over to the British Museum on his return, the captain may have had second thoughts when he failed to find the island again on his return trip. He may have concluded that, rather than risk ridicule at the hands of an incredulous press, it would be better simply to sell them quietly on the side as the "Egyptian relics" the newspaper account said they so closely resembled. If this is so, then it is remotely possible that evidence of a lost civilization reposes today in some unsuspecting antique collector's display case or dusty storage vault quietly awaiting rediscovery.